Cousins In The War

Russell J. Ottens

Published by Russell J. Ottens, 2023.

This is a work of fiction. Similarities to real people, places, or events are entirely coincidental.

COUSINS IN THE WAR

First edition. August 14, 2023.

Copyright © 2023 Russell J. Ottens.

ISBN: 979-8223659723

Written by Russell J. Ottens.

I dedicate this book to the God who created me and has blessed me beyond my wildest imaginings.

Prologue

This is a work of fiction based on fact. Beginning in the late 1980's, I started researching my family history. My mother had told me that my great grandfather was a soldier in the Civil War and that was about all I knew until my thirties. Then I learned that Joseph Seiders served in Co. A, 172nd Drafted Pennsylvania Militia and Co. H, 187th Pennsylvania Volunteer Infantry. I discovered that he was wounded at the Battle of Petersburg on June 18, 1864. I also discovered that two days later, his first cousin, Daniel Seal, Jr., was killed at Kennesaw Mountain in Georgia while serving with Co. E, 1st Missouri Confederate Cavalry (Dismounted). The two cousins met each other in the summer of 1850 when Daniel and his parents made a visit to Pennsylvania. Joseph's mother, Mary Jane Miller Seiders (1810-1872), and Daniel's mother, Catharine Miller Seal (1808-1884), were sisters. I don't know how they got along in 1850, but about the same time I uncovered this information, I felt God leading me to write a novel based on what I knew. It was fascinating that my own ancestors served on opposing sides in the Civil War. There were certainly a multitude of cases of brothers serving on opposite sides, so a story about cousins in the same situation intrigued me.

Chapter One - First Departure

The rolling land of Powell's Valley was painted with brilliant autumn leaves, bathed by early morning sunlight from a cloudless Pennsylvania sky. Blankets of mist still covered the fields that had only recently offered a bountiful harvest. On this beautiful day in late October of 1862, three brothers walked down a lane leaving their boyhood home behind. They were lean, tanned lads who were now abandoning their farm chores, about to embark on what they expected to be a great adventure that could possibly cost them their very lives. The Seiders boys, Joseph, Israel, and William, were headed off to war. For a year and a half, their only contact with the raging conflict had been through newspaper accounts, letters from their cousin Daniel Seal, and an occasional contact with a soldier home on furlough. Less than two months earlier, their eldest brother, John, had volunteered with the 127th Pennsylvania Infantry, leaving his wife and three children behind. The draft had taken these three younger brothers, leaving their 56 year-old father with no sons at home to tend the farm.

The previous spring, Lemuel Harris, a friend from a neighboring farm, had come home with a missing leg. He seemed resigned to his handicap, even relieved that one leg was all he lost. Shortly after his return, Lemuel told Joseph that he planned to continue with his barrel-making and he felt he could be as successful as any two-legged cooper. He had stared into the jaws of death and was thankful to return home to tell about it. Still, Joseph was sickened with the thought that should he serve, he too might lose a limb, or even worse. Like their older brother John, Lemuel had volunteered. Since Joseph, Israel, and William were being drafted, they wouldn't have to blame themselves if any of them came home minus an extremity. On such a beautiful and exciting day, Joseph decided to force all such thoughts out of his head. The air was crisp and clear and he was keenly aware of all the familiar smells of the farm, smells that just never seemed as intense in all his previous years of labor and play. Pungent aromas stroked his olfactory.

There was soil that had just been turned, neatly stacked hay, and of course, the ever-present manure from cows, mules, and horses. With the exception of a trip to Missouri as well as an occasional night at the homes of grandparents, aunts, and uncles, this would be the first time Joseph would be leaving the farm for an extended period of time. After all, he was 21 now, and leaving home was probably an overdue rite of passage. Like it or not, he and his brothers would be serving with the 172nd Pennsylvania Drafted Militia for the next 9 months.

Their father, Henry Seiders, had given all the boys a firm handshake and a stern warning to remember who they were and who was their Lord and Master. Their mother, Mary, embraced each one. For a moment, Joseph had thought her face had aged beyond her 50 years. There were deep furrows in her forehead he hadn't noticed before. Tears fell and her chin quivered. The departure was particularly difficult for Israel. At age 24, he was a widower with a one year-old baby girl. He had traveled with Joseph all the way to Missouri in 1860 to visit their cousins. While there he fell in love with a beautiful young girl who'd been born in England, married, and planned to start a farm in close proximity to his aunt, uncle, and cousins, one of whom named Daniel Seal was now serving in the Confederate army. Israel's wife died a few months after the birth of their daughter. Though devastated, he felt God leading him to return with his daughter to his Pennsylvania home. Only by His grace did Israel and baby Mary complete the perilous journey. Traveling such a distance in 1861 was primitive and fraught with danger. Israel knew his precious little Mary would be safe in the care of her grandparents, but he wondered if he'd ever look upon her cherubic face again. His brothers kissed their little niece, then Israel gave one last kiss to the soft little cheek that he'd kissed a few thousand times before. It was too much to comprehend that at least nine months would pass before he'd have a similar opportunity, that is, *if* he lived to return. Tears streamed down his face as he joined his two brothers headed down a path their feet had trod hundreds of times previously.

The split rail fences became guiding arrows and the natural arch of the fiery maples now appeared to the brothers like a portal to a new world. Golden leaves gently falling before them conjured up images of treasure to be found in some exotic land. About a hundred yards along, Joseph turned for one more look at his parents. His mother was leaning on his father and she returned his wave with her handkerchief in her hand. It was an image he'd see frequently in the future, both in dreams and daytime reveries. Gus, their twelve year-old farm mutt, followed them about two hundred yards more, then stopped and barked a few times. The barking turned to whimpers as he paced from one side of the lane to the other, finally trotting back on arthritic legs to the elder Seiders who were now making their way back to the house. The boys knew with near certainty they'd never lay eyes on Gus again. For that matter, it was possible they'd never see their parents again. Israel wiped his eyes with his sleeve and the three brothers walked along lost in thought, exchanging few words for the next two hours.

Though their destination was less than 20 miles away, there were many steep hills to climb and it was almost dark before they reached Camp Curtin in Harrisburg. The place was bustling with activity. Supply wagons were coming and going and the sound of locomotive bells and whistles filled the air. They were greeted by a pair of stern sentinels who didn't seem the least bit thankful that the Union Army now had three new recruits. In fact, they were downright gruff as they pointed the brothers in the direction of their new regiment. Papers were signed and before the day was over, some officers had thoroughly impressed upon them the idea that obedience to orders was to be paramount in their lives from thence forward. They were now like prisoners in this place and leaving was not permissible without a pass. An officer's order was to be obeyed immediately and without question. Disobedience would have catastrophic consequences.

They spent the night in a small A-frame tent, each wrapped in a single wool blanket that had been issued to them courtesy of the

Commonwealth of Pennsylvania. The brothers arose early after a fitful sleep. They were always up before dawn home on the farm and they felt strange realizing their routine chores were now a thing of the past. There was no doubt their own beds were far more comfortable, but they were thankful they'd been given a small measure of shelter.

After a breakfast that was no match for their mother's culinary skills, they were issued blue uniforms. The fit was less than perfect, but Joseph felt a sense of pride. He was now wearing a military uniform and suddenly was more like his great grandfather, Philip Christian Enders, a man who'd been a Captain in General George Washington's Continental Army. The brothers had heard stories of their ancestor's military prowess, both in the New World and his native Germany. Now they too would be serving their country.

That initial excitement was quickly replaced by the routine of military drill. As the days passed, the brothers got to know some of their comrades at arms. Some of them were even second or third cousins. Some were city dwellers from Harrisburg whose upbringing had been quite different from that of the Seiders boys. For the most part, they got along well with them, but there were a few who looked at life in a totally different manner than the three brothers who'd rarely missed a Sunday in church. The Bible was an integral part of their lives and all of them found it odd that some of their comrades would tease them for reading it in their free time between drilling.

Less than two weeks after their arrival, they were introduced to some new comrades of the six-legged variety. Lice made themselves at home in the Seiders clothing, feasting upon each of the brothers with great gusto. The boys fought them as best they could, but within days they were resigned to the knowledge that soldiers indeed have a lousy life. Like thousands of fellow soldiers, much of the brothers' free time would be devoted to nit-picking along the seams of their uniforms and running lice combs through their hair. Some of their comrades took it all in stride and staged louse races. Two "contestants" would be placed in the middle of a warm frying pan and whoever made it to the edge first was the winner. Though these events were great entertainment, none of the Seiders boys chose to wager on a winner as so many others did. Money was a gift from God too sacred to throw to the wind.

Company drill became a way of life for the Seiders boys. Sometimes they'd be chewed out by their sergeant for not catching on to a particular maneuver fast enough, but most of the time they performed in a satisfactory manner. Joseph began to actually enjoy marching and the mechanical nature of military drill. There was a sense of purpose and a certain pride in being part of a well-oiled machine. Perhaps it was in his blood, Prussian military tradition passed down by his great grandfather, Captain Enders.

Even so, after more than a month of military routine in Camp Curtin, none of the brothers were disappointed to hear the orders given for the 172nd to leave. On December 2, 1862, the regiment marched to the railroad, departed Harrisburg and headed for Washington. Joseph had ridden a train only once before on his 1860 trip to Missouri with his brother Israel. Joseph had previously seen these technological marvels on occasional visits to Harrisburg as a teenager and they never failed to awe him. A massive machine was about to transport him far from the drudgery and regimentation of his training camp. It seemed like a living, breathing behemoth. Even while standing idle, it panted, hissed, and exhaled black smoke while the orange glow of hot fire radiated from deep within its belly. He couldn't hide a boyish grin on his face as he took a seat by the window near the middle of the fourth car back from the locomotive. Glancing around at the other men, he couldn't fathom how most of them could be so nonchalant with the whole experience. It they were not yet veteran soldiers, they appeared to be veteran train travelers.

The train lurched forward and the rhythmic exhaust of the engine barked faster and faster. Joseph waved until the last of the civilian onlookers disappeared from view and the big city of Harrisburg could no longer be seen. It seemed unbelievable that within what seemed like only a few minutes, the train and all its passengers were now hurtling down two iron rails at a high rate of speed. The steady clickety-clack of the wheels over the rail joints was accompanied by frequent blasts on a deep, throaty steam whistle. An occasional metallic squeal as they rounded a curve punctuated the surreal musical concerto. Staring at the passing countryside from the coach window was like traveling in a moving house. Now and then, he could see the locomotive hard at work as the track rounded a sharp curve. His excitement was dampened by some boisterous conversation behind him. Turning around, he saw four of his comrades deeply involved in a card game. How on earth could anybody think of such frivolity when the adventure of a lifetime was in progress? Two seats in front of him, another soldier was similarly excited by the novelty of train travel. It was Zeb Klinger, a boy from a farm about two miles from Joseph's. He had pulled out his pocket watch and was registering the time between mileposts. "Great goodness!," Zeb exclaimed, "That one was just under two minutes! Less than two minutes! Do ya know what that means?? We're movin' over thirty miles an hour! Over thirty miles an hour! Can ya believe it?" The card players were unimpressed, but for Joseph it was a thrill that sped up his heart rate. He once heard a discussion between two very mechanical, well-educated men at a horse auction concerning the future of train travel. They both agreed there were certainly limits to how fast these machines could travel. If a person ever reached a speed of 60 miles per hour, he'd quickly have the air sucked out of his lungs and would suffocate. The thought had a sobering effect on Joseph's train-induced excitement. What if the engineer was fool enough to attempt such velocity on this trip? Joseph took a few deep breaths just to be certain his pulmonary function was in proper order. Good. No ill effects yet. Though he continued to revel in the excitement of it all, he decided a prayer for the safety of himself and all aboard the train certainly couldn't hurt.

Less than two hours into the trip, there was a fifteen minute water stop. The men were ordered to remain in their seats and a small crowd of civilians began conversations through the open coach windows. A small boy of about ten years hollered up to Joseph, "Ya really think ya can whip them Rebs? My big brother says he ain't so sure. He wrote me a letter from Tennessee sayin' he ain't so sure. He said it was nothin' like what he thought it'd be and he just ain't so sure. Wadda ya think?" Without a moment's hesitation, Joseph replied, "Well sure we can!" He heard a laugh from one of the card players behind him. "Hey feller, you'd sure make a good genral! Maybe I can win ya a fancy ossifer suit and a nice pine box to go with it." The boy thought it was funny, but Joseph didn't appreciate the humor. Three teenaged girls came by passing out small pies to the soldiers. Joseph couldn't help but notice their pretty smiles as he and his brothers thanked them profusely. After just a few bites, the four card players made marriage proposals to all three of the lovely maidens. Knowing one would be left out, they began arguing about who offered the most as a potential husband. The teenagers giggled and with a long blast of the whistle, the train came back to life and they waved goodbye to their spouses-to-be. Five hours later, the train reached its destination, a huge encampment near Washington. It didn't seem like a seven-hour trip to Joseph, but he was thankful to once again feel the motionless earth beneath his feet. The company made its way beside the track toward the point of assembly. Joseph slowed his steps as he walked past the resting locomotive. The great monster seemed alive, panting and hissing like a large beast regaining its strength before another assault on the rolling countryside.

The train pulled away shortly after Company A fell in for roll call. It was difficult for Joseph to forget the freedom of the train ride now that he was back under the thumb of his officers. He came back to reality as he heard the name of William Snyder called three times in a row. The first sergeant was losing his temper now as he began to realize the man had disappeared. Inquiries among the corporals and privates who knew him were fruitless. Private Snyder was gone and no one seemed to know where. Joseph hardly knew him, except that he was a city boy from Harrisburg and didn't smile or speak much. Was he a deserter? Maybe it was a legitimate reason that could be excused. Joseph hated to think what might happen to the poor fellow if he was caught. But then, if he was a professional at this sort of thing, he'd deserve it. There were many charlatans who would enlist for the bounty money, only to desert at the earliest opportunity and then re-enlist under another name. What unthinkable thievery!

That first night in the new camp, Joseph stared at the tent above him after his brothers had fallen asleep. The sounds of the train ride replayed in his ears and after drifting off, he enjoyed the ride all over again in his dreams.

The 172nd spent two nights in the camp near Washington. It was sobering to think that decisions regarding the movements of the Union Army were coming in and out of this place. From their current location, the Pennsylvania men could see the Capitol Dome under construction. Soon they were moved to Newport News, Virginia and just a few days later to Yorktown. They settled in for garrison duty that would continue until June of 1863. Camp life here was much the same as in Camp Curtin with an occasional march of 20 miles or more with the possibility of encountering the enemy. It never seemed to happen, but it broke the monotony of constant drilling. The weather was often less than ideal on many of these maneuvers, and occasionally, it was downright miserable. A cold rain might start slowly, then become progressively heavier. Any sensible civilian would seek cover in a warm home, but Joseph and his brothers were no longer sensible civilians. They were soldiers who had to follow orders. Cold water would drip down the back of their necks. The drip would turn into a stream that would soak their shirts and eventually run down the back of their legs. Their shoes would be covered with mud and their socks thoroughly soaked. There was no escape from the torment and the boys would stoically resign themselves to their soggy fate. The wet wool of their sack coats gave off an unpleasant smell. Daydreams about the smell of baking bread and apple pies right out of the oven could chase it away for a short while, but it would always come back. By the time they'd return to camp, they'd be chilled to the bone. Upon returning to their tent, they'd change into dry shirts and socks, then wrap themselves in a blanket, shivering uncontrollably until a fitful sleep would mercifully remove them from their misery. The misery returned when the bugler blew reveille and it was time to put the soggy sack coat and wool pants back on. Through it all, the Seiders brothers tried to stay positive. Their parents had taught them to give thanks in all situations and look for God's blessings in everything.

Chapter Two - Joseph's Illness in Camp

It had been over a month now since the men had learned of a terrible defeat of the Union Army at Fredericksburg. Joseph heard firsthand accounts of the carnage on that cold December day, enough to make him reconsider his eagerness for experiencing his first battle. One veteran he spoke with had lost two fingers on his left hand.

Though his experience with the 172nd had been monotonous for the most part, he was thankful he wasn't a gruesome statistic from the horrors of the Fredericksburg fiasco. It seemed hard to imagine his first cousin, Daniel Seal, living through so very many engagements unscathed. The war had been raging almost two years and Daniel had seen major action at Wilson's Creek in Missouri, Iuka and Corinth in Mississippi and dozens of other fights of a smaller scale. Letters from his mother's sister, Aunt Catharine, kept Joseph informed of Daniel's experiences. About two weeks after New Year's Day, he received one written to him by Daniel himself. It was dated October 5, 1862 and had been sent first to Daniel's mother in Missouri, then to Joseph's mother in Pennsylvania, then to Joseph in Virginia. He hadn't seen his cousin Daniel since the fall of 1860 when he left Missouri after his brother's wedding. Daniel and Joseph had a special bond. How he wished he could have traveled to Missouri to help his brother Israel return to Pennsylvania after his wife died, but his father had insisted he stay on the farm. The Seiders family was very thankful when Israel returned safely with his precious baby daughter. Though Israel was grieving, it was good to have his help on the farm and baby Mary melted every Seiders heart. Frequently, Joseph would pump Israel for information about cousin Daniel, life in Missouri, and his journey back to Pennsylvania with the baby.

Here at the winter camp in Yorktown, Joseph became seriously ill for the first time since early childhood. He had experienced an occasional cold, but nothing that kept him from his daily farm chores. Now, like many of the men in his regiment, he was too sick to report for roll call. It started with achiness throughout his body during drill on a cold afternoon with a persistent wet snowfall. He tried to ignore it and was able to have supper with his messmates. He got in his tent as early as he could, extremely thankful that he didn't have picket duty that night. He kept all his clothes on, including his coat, removing only his shoes. Huddled under his blanket, he shivered uncontrollably. His jaw soon became sore as he clamped it tightly shut to keep his teeth from chattering. Amid the familiar chorus of conversation, coughs, and laughter from the men outside, he dozed into a light sleep, only to be awakened by intense nausea. Crawling halfway out of the tent, he heaved all his supper, his last solid food for the next week. He crawled back in the tent, exhausted with cold sweat on his brow. The chills returned and kept him half awake until the first gray light painted the outline of Israel's sleeping form beside him. Israel had picket duty that night and Joseph didn't notice him come in. Soon the bugler blew reveille. Israel mumbled a few complaints and was up in less than a minute, in spite of his lack of sleep. For the first time since being drafted, Joseph couldn't get up. His words came out slow and feebly. "Send the sarge my regrets, I think I caught something and I just can't make it this morning." "Sure Joe," replied his tent mate and brother, "just promise me you won't die. Promise me, cuz it would be awful to die in a war without ever firin' a shot!" Joseph gave a nod and as Israel exited the tent, he could see that it was snowing drier and heavier than the day before. He felt sick enough to welcome death, knowing to be absent from the body would bring him into the presence of his Lord. He knew his passing would be hard on his parents and his brothers, so he prayed they might be comforted if the event was to be God's will.

At noon, his brother William came by with a tin cup full of hot coffee. Joseph was one of three odd men in the company who just didn't drink it. Most of the soldiers considered their coffee ration equally precious as food. Joseph didn't like the taste and he didn't like the idea of drinking something scalding hot. At first he refused William's offer, but his brother insisted it was necessary to warm him up and get some strength. Joseph took a few small sips. Israel found him another blanket. For the next two days, Joseph alternated between shivers and sweats, hardly able to eat or drink much of anything. His brothers took turns looking after him when the duties of the day were through. Frequently they'd run a louse comb through his hair to banish a few of his tormentors. In a way, just the fact that they were there was a good sign. Once a soldier died in camp, the ever loyal lice would desert the cold body by the hundreds, like an army in full retreat.

The Seiders boys had been raised to believe in the power of prayer and they did so audibly as Joseph slipped in and out of sleep. One day, Israel was able to trade off some coffee for a cup of chicken broth, a rare commodity in camp. Surely this was provided by God's loving hands. Two days after drinking the broth, Joseph woke up just before dawn drenched in sweat. His fever had finally broken and he was thirsty enough to take more than the usual few sips from his canteen. His appetite was back and he eagerly consumed a small piece of hardtack that had spent a lonely week in his haversack. After morning parade, Joseph was happy to reunite with his mess mates. They were glad to see he'd recovered. As was their custom since they began army life, one of the Seiders brothers blessed the food. This morning it was William. It was twice as long as the usual prayer since he needed to acknowledge God's healing of his brother. All the brothers had seen men removed from their tents as a corpse from similar battles with sickness and they were very thankful Joseph wasn't one of them.

Chapter Three - Flashback to Childhood

Mail call was a welcome break from the routine of army life. Sometimes there were packages from home with food, socks, books, and even photographs. On an unseasonably warm day in late March of 1863, Joseph received a small package. Inside was a small jar of his mother's finest blackberry jam carefully wrapped in three hand-made washcloths. His mother had lovingly stitched the initials of the three brothers on each one. The package also contained a photograph of their cousin, Daniel Seal. Of course, the uniform was Confederate, but if anyone would happen to see it, they probably couldn't tell from the picture and they didn't need to know. His mother's note explained that the picture had been first sent to his Aunt Catharine in Missouri, then passed along to his mother in Pennsylvania. His mother knew how close they'd become when they were boys, and she felt Joseph would appreciate it most. His mind raced back in time to 1850 when he and his cousin shared a storybook summer. Uncle Dan Seal and Aunt Catharine came all the way to Pennsylvania from Missouri, bringing their youngest child with them. Daniel was eight and Joseph was nine. What a summer it was! How could he forget the old hen that insisted on attacking Daniel whenever he approached within ten feet. The first morning he had attempted to retrieve her egg, this determined chicken decided she just didn't like Missouri boys. After several unsuccessful attempts, Daniel finally got it, but the sight of the infuriated fowl chasing him through the barn and out the side door left Joseph rolling on the ground in hysteria. Daniel didn't quite see the humor in it, and the two were soon locked in an impromptu wrestling match. When Daniel delivered a punch to his stomach, Joseph responded with a fist to his right eye.

The wounded Missouri boy ran back to the house crying. The young Pennsylvanian considered hiding somewhere, but his father was too much of a disciplinarian, and he decided to head for the house and accept the inevitable. Upon arriving Joseph found his mother and aunt tending to the eye that was rapidly swelling closed.

The stern voice of his mother fell upon his ears. "Son, how could you do this to my sister's child when they traveled a thousand miles to see us and haven't been here two days yet? If your father wasn't so busy harnessing the mules, your hind quarters would be blistered! Now, fetch my spoon so I can do the job."

A few quick swats with the wooden utensil out on the front steps and it was all over. The sting brought tears, but he was thankful the iron hand of his father wasn't the instrument of readjustment. Back inside, the two boys were soon listening to Aunt Catharine reading the story of Cain and Abel from the family Bible. God spoke to Joseph through those words and the sense of remorse he felt for hurting his own flesh and blood was overwhelming.

A strong bond was formed between the two cousins that day, one that would last the rest of their life. Joseph told Daniel how truly sorry he was and the bond was sealed with a tearful embrace. They didn't notice, but their mothers had some tears to wipe away also. From that day forward, they were inseparable and never fought again. With young Daniel's help, Joseph's chores went much faster and seemed much more tolerable. They were quite often accompanied by laughs and giggles.

Thanks to Daniel, there was much more free time. Countless carefree hours were spent in boyhood adventure. There were frogs to catch, butterflies to chase, and a pet box turtle named General Washington who feasted on crickets and wild berries. What fun it was to wade in the cool waters of the creek on a hot July day, turning over rocks in search of crayfish. A hemlock tree became a crow's nest on a pirate ship where the boys imagined that the beautiful view of Powell's Valley was a vast ocean full of ships loaded with treasure. The supper bell would ring way too soon, but there was usually time to catch fireflies afterward.

In early August there was a particular day when a steady rain kept everyone inside. Mary Seiders allowed Joseph and Daniel to make their own little teepee with a blanket thrown over a small table. The cousins spent the day alternating between pow-wows in their cozy new dwelling and stalking buffalo throughout every room in the house. Aunt Catharine even helped fashion Indian headdresses with scraps of fabric and a few feathers plucked from an old duster. Henry Seiders played the part of a rogue buffalo putting his index fingers to each side of his head and charging the young Indian braves.

On one beautiful evening with an overabundance of fireflies, Daniel asked his Aunt Mary for a jar. Joseph asked what it was for and he explained his new invention. They could both fill it with about a hundred fireflies and then they'd have a brilliant lamp to light their path. Soon the jar had so many, it was hard to keep those already captured from escaping. The boys were disappointed that the fireflies wouldn't co-operate with them to make the new invention a success. Once inside the jar, most of the insects simply quit shining their light. When they gave the sad news to Daniel's father, he was sympathetic and offered some great wisdom. "Boys, it's too bad your new invention didn't work. For now we'll have to stick to this one." He lifted his kerosene lantern slightly and continued. "Ya know, this lamp does a pretty good job, but do ya know what's even better?" Joseph quickly blurted, "A torch?" "Nope. The Bible!" The two cousins glanced at each other quizzically. "The Bible says 'Thy Word is a lamp unto my feet and a light unto my path.' Promise me you'll both always remember that, even when you're all grown up like me." The light of his lamp brought them both back to the house. They'd remember those words for the rest of their lives. After being tenderly tucked in bed by the two sisters that gave them birth, the two cousins quickly drifted off to sleep on the soft feather mattress. Both had wonderful dreams that reran many of the summer's adventures. It was hard to leave that warm bed on cool mornings when Papa Seiders woke them before dawn to begin their chores!

Far too quickly, the days grew noticeably shorter and the air became perceptibly cooler. The boys knew that soon, Daniel would be returning to Missouri with his parents. The katydids were singing now whenever the evening darkness arrived. Their music drifted in to the boys' room through the open window. It was the last sound they'd hear each night before they'd drift off to sleep. Every August and September thereafter, the song of the katydids reminded both Joseph and Daniel of the magical summer of 1850.

One late August afternoon, they decided that being cousins was just not enough. They needed to be blood brothers. Just how to go about it took some thinking, however. Daniel found the solution when he remembered how blackberry thorns often drew blood on their foraging expeditions. With as much bravery as can be mustered by two young boys, they pricked their index fingers on a convenient bush and exchanged blood. Now they would always be close, even if over a thousand miles were between them.

The Seals left on the 11th day of September, an extremely difficult day for Joseph. Adding to the sadness was the fact that Joseph's Grandmother, Christina, would be leaving Pennsylvania and going with the Seals to Missouri. Her husband, John Miller, had died the summer before and Christina felt a new life in Missouri would ease her grief. There were many hugs, kisses, and kind words exchanged that day, but none could remove the lump in Joseph's throat. Aunt Catharine reassured him that it wouldn't be so bad, both boys knew how to write and they could keep in touch with letters. She wiped the tears from his eyes and hugged him one last time. She didn't have to do that for Joseph's brothers. John and Israel were quite a bit older, William was younger, and they just didn't have the bond that had grown between Daniel and Joseph. The Seiders had a portrait of their grandmother, so she told Joseph to look at it now and then so he wouldn't forget her. He tearfully said he could never forget her, even without the picture. Little did he know that she'd be in Heaven in just over a year.

He followed the wagon along for nearly half a mile until the lump in his throat seemed almost too big to breathe. The sight of them leaving the farm in a trail of dust was etched in Joseph's mind, though it became blurred once he stopped and a flood of tears filled his eyes. He had to retreat to the crow's nest in the hemlock tree to gather his thoughts and deal with his grief. It was nearly dark when he heard his mother calling him to supper. He didn't have much of an appetite, but he did the best he could to finish his meal. Harvest chores helped take his mind off his summer companion, but the times they shared would never be forgotten.

Daniel was a good little traveler for the first two days of the trip home, but after supper on the second night, he broke down in tears. "I want to go back, I just want to go back!," he wailed. They were over 50 miles from Powell's Valley. His father sternly rebuked him, saying it was impossible now. Besides, they were going home to Missouri whether he liked it or not. His mother was more understanding, cradling him in her arms while trying to soothe his hurt. "Daniel, there are times we have to leave the ones we love. It was just a few years back when your big sister, Mary, had to say goodbye to the teacher she loved so very much. Remember how she followed the wagon as long as she could, crying all the way?" "She never came back!," Daniel blurted. "That's true, son, and Mary still misses her, but they write letters and someday they'll have a reunion." Daniel's sobbing had slowed down some now, and as he tried to regain his composure, he asked, "What's a reunion?" His mother stroked his hair. "A reunion is when people who love each other get together after being apart." Daniel paused to gather his thoughts. "Well how do you know Mary will see her teacher again?" Catharine held her son's cheeks in her hands. "Mary may not see her teacher again in this life, but I know for certain she will in Heaven. The Bible tells us this and I believe it with all my heart, just like I believe you'll see

Joseph again. It may not be here on earth, but if not, I know we'll all see him in Heaven. What a wonderful day that will be, when once again we see all those we've loved so much here on earth. Think of how much it will mean to me to see Grandpa John, my father who you never got to meet. Remember how happy I was to see my mother when we first got to Aunt Mary's house?" Daniel thought his mother was confused. "You weren't happy, you were crying!" "Tears don't have to be sad, we can cry happy tears, and believe me, when I saw your grandmother, I was happier than you could ever imagine. But it doesn't matter. Someday, God will wipe away all our tears." Catharine wiped away the last of Daniel's tears. He squeezed her tightly. "It's been a long day and it's time for a little boy to get to sleep." The big, strong arms of Daniel's father picked him up and tucked him into his bedroll in the corner of the wagon. He didn't say a word, but he kissed his son on the cheek and pulled his blanket up to both ears. A great feeling of peace came over him. As he looked into the perfectly clear night sky, the beautiful orange streak of a shooting star was the last thing he saw before he closed his eyes in sleep.

The cousins would see each other one more time when Joseph traveled to Missouri with his brother Israel. It was good to see Daniel once again. At age 18, Daniel had grown a little taller than his cousin Joseph who was one year older. The childhood play times were a thing of the past, but they were still close and had much to talk about while Joseph helped Daniel on the Seal farm. His Aunt Catharine had aged a lot over the last ten years, but she was just as sweet and loving as in the summer of 1850. Daniel's father had died in 1852, but when it happened, all of her children were grown except Daniel. His older siblings gave Daniel's mother great comfort during her time of loss. Joseph considered settling in Missouri, but he felt he needed to make his life in his native state of Pennsylvania. After Israel married, Joseph bid farewell to Missouri and the Seal Family. It wasn't as hard to leave Cousin Daniel as it was when they were children. Winds of war were blowing when he left. Shortly after his return to Pennsylvania, South Carolina left the Union. Back in Missouri, folks were divided. Some wanted to join South Carolina and some didn't. Although Missouri was a slave state, it remained in the Union, though a large portion of its inhabitants wanted it out. A convention of Southern sympathizers set up a separate government calling for secession and statehood in the Confederacy. Bitter fighting erupted with lawless gangs burning homes of those who didn't agree with them, followed by retaliation in kind. The situation spiraled downhill from bad to worse.

Chapter Four - The Vicksburg Trenches

About 600 miles from his cousins stationed in Virginia, Daniel Seal was in Vicksburg, Mississippi. He had been in the war for more than two years now with hardly a month going by that he wasn't part of a major, bloody encounter with blue-coated soldiers. Daniel first served with the Missouri State Guard. About a month after a major engagement against Federal forces at Pea Ridge, Arkansas, he enlisted in Co. E, First Missouri Cavalry (Dismounted) on April 15, 1862. One week earlier, this regiment had its horses requisitioned by orders from Richmond. From that time on, the men fought as infantry. Their double-barrel shotguns were traded for .58 caliber Mississippi rifled muskets. Hundreds upon hundreds of miles of marching lay ahead.

For four days now, Daniel had been here in Vicksburg, but he just couldn't stop thinking about the fiasco at Big Black River the week before. The Yankees had burned the railroad bridge over this meandering tributary that eventually flowed into the Mississippi. Confronted with overwhelming numbers of Yankee soldiers, his regiment somehow had to retreat to the west bank. The screams of his drowning comrades still echoed in his head. Daniel couldn't shake the sounds from his ears, even though he was a good swimmer and was able to get across safely. He actually swam toward a floundering boy who may not have been even 18 years old. He was crying out in hysteria and just as Daniel came within ten yards, the boy vanished beneath the muddy waters. Daniel continued swimming and dove down twice in a futile attempt to rescue this child warrior, but he could only see a curtain of solid brown as he opened his eyes and his outstretched arms touched nothing. Back on the surface, he made for the western shore, swimming around occasional chunks of debris from the blown bridge. Upon reaching the bank, he turned and looked toward the place where the boy had gone under. A sick, hollow feeling invaded the pit of his stomach as he contemplated the young life that had been snuffed out just moments earlier. If only he had swum just slightly faster, the boy might be standing beside him now. It was too much for Daniel and he started to cry.

"Reform your ranks! For God's sake, reform your ranks!" Daniel knew he had to pull himself together and get back with what remained of his company. He climbed the steep, briar-laden embankment and ran through the woods. He emerged into a field of young corn, much of which had been hopelessly trampled. Daniel always hated to see food go to waste and he hated seeing portions of someone's corn field destroyed by something as senseless as war. Eventually he caught up with his comrades. Many of the men had lost their weapons crossing the river. Those who made it across earlier, before the bridge was destroyed, still had theirs and were firing sporadically in a rearguard action. Some of these defenders had been hit and those without rifles picked them up from the dead and wounded. Daniel found an abandoned Enfield and took it with him, but he'd have to find some dry ammunition since his cartridge box was thoroughly soaked. Shortly he found a wounded man of about forty lying on his back motionless. Daniel instinctively reached for his canteen to give him some water, but it was gone. Maybe the strap had been torn as he retreated with his comrades. "I know ... I know it's mortal," came the strained words from his cracked lips. Blood trickled down his right cheek. "I know this is it. I'm fixin' to die, but I ain't Heaven-bound, I know I ain't. It's dark, it's cold, it ain't Heaven. It ain't, d-mmit! It ain't! I'm headed to hell, I jest know it!!" Daniel replied, "Hush, now, don't say that! You don't have to go there. I can pray with you right now."

"I done too much bad in my life, just too dern much. They ain't no takin' back the wicked things I done. I can't ... ," Blood foamed from his mouth and his words were choked off. He was gasping with a look of sheer panic on his face.

"No! No, there's no reason you can't let Jesus take your sins away, right here, right now. Even the thief on the cross next to Jesus was able to go to Heaven! You can go ... ," A frenzied hand grabbed Daniels hair, as if it were grabbing at a slender root poking out from the edge of a cliff. The nameless soldier then clamped his fist so tightly, some of Daniel's hair pulled out. As he reached to dislodge it, the arm suddenly went limp and hit the ground. Kneeling at his side, Daniel couldn't help but notice his eyes. They stared right at him and burned a permanent image in Daniel's mind. He was dead, but the eyes told the whole story. This man had just departed this earthly life and now was completely and forever removed from God's love! Daniel paused for some thirty seconds, mourning the loss of someone who was a total stranger to him. He then started running, though in short order he realized that he'd forgotten all about the cartridges! He stopped, turned, and looked toward the lifeless body. Once again, he saw the eyes as if they were face to face. He'd find cartridges elsewhere. Somehow, Daniel survived the Battle of Big Black River. Only a God-given miracle had gotten him through it.

A loud burst from a shell just 100 feet in front of their line shook Daniel back to the present. He was back in his muddy trench where he knew death could come at any moment. For Daniel, that was not a frightening thought. He knew where he was going if he were to die, but he couldn't stop thinking of the boy and the man at Big Black River. He knew where the man was and the thought just sickened him. He wasn't sure about the boy. He hoped that he was a Christian, but it haunted him that in this life, he'd never know. If only he'd reached them both sooner! If only!

The shelling grew more intense now. The Missouri boys had been ordered to keep their rate of fire very slow to conserve ammunition, but the musketry from both sides was becoming louder and more rapid. In the mud of the trench for several days now, the situation had become worse. Dead and dying soldiers were everywhere and the sounds of battle were heard continuously. During an occasional lull in the fighting, it seemed surreal to hear birds singing. How could they be so oblivious to the harsh reality of war? Their music was absolutely beautiful. Daniel decided that surely this was the voice of God giving comfort to any soldier who might listen.

Like most of the men in his unit, Daniel adjusted to the filth and monotony of life in the trenches quite rapidly. Civilized people would find it hard to imagine sleeping with a steady rain assaulting your body, waking at first light knee-deep in mud. The stench of dead soldiers, horses, and human excrement was horrible, but a man could get used to it fairly quickly. Sleep came at intervals. Sometimes, the steady din of artillery would lull Daniel into sleep, only to come to an abrupt halt when a shell crashed way too close. It was during one of these fitful sleeps that he had a dream he'd carry with him the rest of his life. A battle commenced with musket and cannon shots fired from both sides. Shells began whistling through the air and screams of wounded and dying men grew steadily louder. Suddenly, birds appeared in the sky. They were pure white and as they came closer to the ground, he saw they weren't birds at all, but angels! Strangely, men from both sides began shooting at them. Daniel shouted at the top of his lungs for them to cease firing, but the firing continued unabated. Some of the angels began flying very low, just barely above the ground. Daniel attempted to catch one, without success. All of them appeared adult-sized, but when a small one passed, he was quick enough to grab it. He stared at it and saw what appeared to be a beautiful seven year-old girl with golden hair filled with curls. While holding her, she seemed very frightened, her heart beating rapidly and her wings fluttering like a captured bird. "Please, calm down, I won't hurt you, I promise!," he said. "Why are you here?" A beautiful child's voice answered, "Because you must stop hurting each other." Suddenly Daniel awoke, his heart pounding and his shirt collar dampened with sweat. What was that? What did it mean? He glanced up and down the dark, muddy trench. All the soldiers appeared to be sleeping. Apparently, the angels didn't fly into their dreams. Was the little angel his sister, Annie Jane, who died at age seven? It could have been her face, but he just wasn't sure. She died when Daniel wasn't quite four. He couldn't remember much about her except that she was always protective of him, cuddling him like she was the mama and he was the baby. When she became ill, his parents told him to pray for Annie and he didn't even know what that meant. His heart slowed down and he tried to review all the dream's details. So just what was the meaning of his dream? He let out a sigh and thought for a moment. Well it was obvious what it meant! This whole war was insane and God didn't want the slaughter to continue. Now that he had his dream figured out, why not tell it to the generals and let them take the necessary action? Why not? Why not just wake up everyone, tell them he'd gone mad and it was time to be sent back to Missouri?

Daniel straightened up from the knurled position in which he'd been sleeping. Everything was eerily quiet and a thousand stars shone from above. He looked to the west and found that the crescent moon had set while he was asleep. Indeed he'd had a remarkable dream and he replayed it in his head several times. Would he tell anyone? Probably not or he'd be laughed at mercilessly.

With the onset of daylight, the shelling and musketry resumed. For two more days, the bitter fighting continued. Daniel just followed orders and kept up the firing. He couldn't see the big picture, but God could. Looking down, the two armies would appear to Him as thousands of little blue and gray ants fighting one another. Daniel remembered watching a column of ants with his cousin Joseph in 1850. He had drawn his foot across them and the ants had stopped, backing up as if suddenly blocked by an invisible wall. Why couldn't God just draw his foot across the hillside at Vicksburg and suddenly pry the blue and gray armies totally apart?

When darkness fell on May 21st, the bombardment of Vicksburg didn't cease. Shells poured in from Union gunboats on the Mississippi throughout the night. The dawn of May 22nd was eerily quiet until the sounds of murderous shells ushered in the daylight. During a brief lull in the fighting, Daniel heard someone's rooster crow. He wondered how much longer that bird would live before he became someone's meal. Food was already getting scarce as supply wagons couldn't reach the soldiers. The thought of the rooster reminded him of the chicken chase on the visit to Pennsylvania in 1850. He'd been so mad with his cousin Joseph after he punched his eye, but from that point forward the two had been inseparable. If only he could somehow go back to Pennsylvania that very day, a day when he was still blissfully ignorant of the sounds of war. He felt the cheek below his right eye, just to be sure all the pain of his cousin's well-directed punch of thirteen years ago was gone. Suddenly, a shell landing less than fifty yards to his left broke his reverie. He heard groans and screams worse than any he'd heard previously. This assault seemed like the worst yet. How could it go on for hours and hours without end? It did go on and the assault only intensified as the day wore on. General Grant was holding nothing back.

Suddenly, there was a bright blue flash and Daniel was knocked to the ground. A shell fragment had struck his right eye. He felt a wave of nausea, then passed out.

Chapter Five - Eye Hath Not Seen

A bright flash of lightning illuminated the inside of the makeshift hospital that had shortly before been someone's stately home. Within a few seconds, a loud thunderclap awakened Daniel. More followed. It was almost a comfort to hear God's thunder rather than the thunder of artillery that brought so much death and destruction. The muffled groans from some of the other wounded around him reminded Daniel of the barrage of the previous day. He was thankful that his pain was more tolerable than most of the other soldiers, even though he now faced life with only one eye.

As he lay there listening to the crashing booms, Daniel was taken back to one of his earliest memories, probably not long after his family moved from Ohio to Missouri. A violent thunderstorm had startled him from his sleep. His heart was pounding with fear and he started to cry. Through the darkness, he toddled across the cabin's wood floor to his parents' bed. His father's strong arms quickly picked him up and placed him snugly in the middle, under the covers. His calm voice was comforting, especially since he showed no fear each time the thunder boomed. Neither did his mother. She softly whispered, "It's alright, Precious, God sees all of us right now and He won't let us get hurt. He loves us so much that nothing can take us away from Him." His father spoke next. "Daniel, the clouds are just bumping into each other. God made the clouds and they do that sometimes. He won't let them carry on like that forever, just you wait and see. He'll calm them down real soon." There was never a time Daniel felt more safe and warm than that night between his mother and father. From that point forward, he knew God was love.

The next morning, as the sun's rays beamed through the hospital window, just as they had through the window of his boyhood cabin back in 1845, he knew God was in control and there was no need to fear. The message was even clearer on this beautiful morning in 1863 than it was the morning after a frightened little boy first learned about who He was. In spite of his horrible wound, he had much to be thankful for. The loss of an eye was bad, but there were soldiers nearby him that were far more horribly mangled. He hadn't lost any limbs and by God's grace, he still had one good eye. God put a verse in his mind, 1 Corinthians 2:9. "*But as it is written, Eye hath not seen, nor ear heard, neither have entered into the heart of man, the things which God hath prepared for them that love him.*" His remaining eye had never seen Heaven, but some day he'd behold it with two perfect eyes. Nothing he'd ever done would be enough to earn his way in, but thanks to Jesus, his entry fee had already been paid.

The day wore on slowly, the sound of artillery ebbed and flowed, and the flies continued their incessant buzz. The air in the hospital hung heavily around his bed. "Lord if only you could provide us a bit of a breeze, I think most of these men would be thankful. I know I would, Dear Lord." His prayer was answered in less than half an hour. Indeed, the wind picked up, enough to push the flies off his face for a few blissful moments. Another period of stillness followed, lasting almost an hour, then came a stronger wind, noticeably cooler than the first. Was it thunder he was hearing now, or more artillery? He couldn't be sure as he drifted off into a light sleep.

He was dreaming now. Just like the dream before his wounding, a battle was beginning once again. This time, when the angels appeared, the men ceased their firing. All was quiet now except for the soft flutter of wings. The same golden-haired little angel arrived again, this time hovering in mid-air before him. She spoke in a sweet and beautiful voice. "It's a long walk home, but you'll get there. You'll get home." Just as before, he awoke with a pounding heart. Surely it was his sister and surely he'd be going home! What joy! It was almost too wonderful to imagine. He pictured his arms around his mother on the front porch of the house in Missouri. His brothers and sisters would crowd around him and the horrors of war would leave him forever!

From that point forward, the days passed quickly. He was thankful for the kind men and women who cared for his wound. His small New Testament provided great comfort during those waking hours when there was sufficient light for his left eye to read and reread its words of truth. In spite of the increasing heat as May turned to June and the situation in Vicksburg grew bleaker, Daniel knew his dream would carry him through whatever hardships lay ahead. One of the hardships was a scarcity of food. All supply from the outside world had been cut off for several weeks now. While recovering from his wound, Daniel's appetite wasn't as great as the soldiers still in the trenches. He could get by on one piece of hard tack per day, though chewing was painful on the side where he'd lost his eye. Sometimes as he shivered with chills or sweated with fever as his body fought against horrible infection, he'd dream of the wonderful mid-day dinners prepared by his mother back on the farm in Missouri. What he wouldn't give for just one narrow slice of her unforgettable apple pie! A bowl of her stewed rhubarb would be a taste of heaven itself! For that matter, just one meal with all his cousins gathered around the table at his Aunt Mary's Pennsylvania house in 1850 would be more precious than a bar of gold. Mashed potatoes with gravy, warm bread with butter, green beans, chicken, apple sauce, and oh those sweet corn fritters! How could he ever have taken such feasts for granted? God had blessed him with good food for most of his 21 years and he prayed for forgiveness for any meal he'd previously eaten without a deep sense of appreciation for the Lord's kindness in providing it. In Sunday School, he memorized the 25th and 26th verse of Psalm 136. *"God giveth food to all flesh: for his mercy endureth for ever. O give thanks unto the God of heaven: for his mercy endureth for ever."* There were so many verses he'd had to memorize when he was a small boy. It seemed like drudgery back then, but now many of those same verses came back to him bringing great joy and comfort in his time of misery. If he ever got back to Missouri, he'd be sure and throw his arms around Miss Ogan, Mrs. Boydston, and Mrs.

Holland for giving their time to him in Sunday School. How could he have taken them for granted? They had loved him even when he was less than angelic. They had served the Lord willingly and Daniel was thankful.

Though the sights and sounds in the hospital were gruesome and pitiful, Daniel gave thanks each day for the outpouring of God's love through his obedient servants. The worst of possible situations was bringing out the very best in many people who denied self and ministered tirelessly to the wounded. Surgeons, nurses, and orderlies went from bed to bed bringing comforts only the Lord could provide. On one particular evening that was hot and muggy, Daniel was visited by a Missouri chaplain who introduced himself as E.M. Bounds. After a few questions that determined Daniel's standing with God, Chaplain Bounds began a delightful conversation. Daniel was amazed to learn this man of God had met his own pastor on more than one occasion. Next came a lengthy prayer that seemed to cover every imaginable request a wounded soldier might have. Pleas for healing, family members, safety, peace, comfort and on and on came forth as the prayer continued. After a while, this servant of the Lord had to move on to the next patient, but Daniel would never forget the power of that prayer in a hot Vicksburg hospital, given in love while the sounds of battle could be heard in the distance.

By the latter part of June, the Confederates were eating mule meat. Daniel was well enough now to be back in the trenches, though his missing eye and the surrounding wound were still not completely healed. His first meal of stewed mule was memorable. The meat was tough and chewing on it brought pain to his wound. Just the thought of eating a mule wasn't pleasant either. Back home on the farm, he'd spent countless hours with mules he considered part of the family. He called them by name and they willingly obeyed his commands. They seemed almost human, eager to please and serve him. Only on rare occasions did they stop and refuse to work. Daniel knew from experience that when they reached that point, nothing could get them moving again, as if they were conscious that they'd reached the limit of their endurance and a desire for self-preservation brought them to a standstill. Now he was eating them, maybe not his family mules, but their distant kin. He was thankful to have any food at all, though, and he prayed that the mules back home in Buchanan County, Missouri were alive and well. In the last letter he'd received from his mother, she spoke of nearby homes and barns burned down in the wretched partisan warfare that had engulfed the whole state for the past two years. Union forces would eagerly set a torch to a home if they suspected any of the tenants had Confederate sympathies. Revenge in kind would be wrought upon pro-Union households and so-on in a never-ending vicious and violent cycle of destruction. The Seal home could easily become a target due to Daniel's Confederate service, but maybe by God's grace they'd have pity on his mother on account of her widowhood. He prayed often for the safety of his mother, brothers and sisters. Fortunately, the Union service of his older brothers kept them close to home, perhaps allowing them to keep a watchful eye on the Seal farm. Oh, how he only wished he could be there! Home. He wanted to go home!

One particular night, a talented soldier in his regiment sang *Lorena*, accompanied by an equally talented fiddler. It was a beautiful song the soldiers loved to hear, though the lyrics told a heart-wrenching story of lost love. He heard it on many previous occasions, but with all he'd been through since leaving home almost two years earlier, the deepest longings of his heart caught up with him. Daniel felt a swelling lump in his throat and emotions gave way. Tears streamed down his face. He may have lost an eye, but all his tear ducts were fully functional. How he longed for home and a reunion with his loved ones. His sobs made breathing difficult and he had to step back from the light of the fire so no one would see. It was an instinctive reaction, though not a necessary one in this situation. Most of his comrades felt the same way and none would have anything derogatory to say since nearly all of them had done the same thing, probably a lot more than once since leaving their own Missouri homes. When he finally regained his composure, he silently thanked the Lord for the multitude of blessings He had sent Daniel's way.

Life was just awful for the men in the Vicksburg trenches, but mercifully, the hardship didn't go on indefinitely. On July 4th, the city surrendered. The artillery fire ceased, exchanged for brilliant fireworks in the night sky, courtesy of the victorious Yankees. He was now their prisoner, but he was confident he'd soon be on his way home. In a matter of days he was exchanged and paroled like all the other Vicksburg Confederates.

Many of the Yankee soldiers took pity on the ragged, hungry soldiers who had defended Vicksburg. It seemed surreal that some of these men in blue were sharing their rations with men the same soldiers they were trying to kill just a few days earlier. Daniel was very thankful at least a portion of these men took the words of Jesus seriously when he gave his Sermon on the Mount. *"Love your enemies."* One kind soldier who shared some food with Daniel was from a Missouri regiment. He lived in Andrew County, which bordered Daniel's Buchanan County. He then introduced Daniel to a young comrade named Bob that hailed from Buchanan County as well. Their conversation lasted over an hour, each cross-checking who they both knew. When Bob was called to leave he put his hand on Daniel's shoulder and gave a short prayer. "Lord, I ask you to watch over my brother Daniel and lead him safely home. Heal his wound and please bring an end to this cruel, sinful war. Forgive us all for the way we've grieved you. In Jesus' name, Amen."

How strange! This war made no sense. Men that could one day be slaughtering each other and another day be comforting each other was too much to comprehend. Thousands upon thousands had been killed or maimed, but for what? Why did sin have to enter the world?

Why did Cain slay his brother Abel? Daniel's home state was divided, his home country was divided and no matter which side emerged victorious, bitter seeds of hatred would sprout weeds of sin for years to come. Only Jesus could repair the damage that had been done. Sadly, Daniel knew there were far too many who didn't believe that.

Though still weak, Daniel could walk and he was overjoyed the day he finally began marching with his regiment out of Vicksburg. At last, they were leaving the place of so much misery and suffering. His joy turned to sadness, however, when he realized the army was not marching back to Missouri. They were headed east. "Lord, how could this be?" thought Daniel, "How could this be after you sent your angels into my dreams?" Though discouraged, he carried the dreams with him, confident he was headed home somehow, even if he and all the other soldiers were marching in the wrong direction.

Eventually, they reached Demopolis, Alabama, where a surgeon dressed his wound. Shortly after he'd finished, Daniel looked to the west to see a brilliant and beautiful sunset with countless shades of orange and red painted on distant clouds. He thanked the Lord that he was blessed with a functional eye able to behold the magnificent scene. Once again, he whispered the verse he'd memorized as a child. *"Eye hath not seen, nor ear heard, neither have entered into the heart of man ..."*

Chapter Six - Picket Duty for Joseph

In the early spring of 1863, all was quiet except for the pleasant choir of spring peepers in the thick, dark woods of Virginia. Joseph Seiders was on picket duty when he was suddenly startled by a voice. "Hey Billy! Can ya hear me?" A pang of panic twisted Joseph's stomach. Should he answer back? The voice was louder now. "Can't ya hear me Billy?" He had to do something, so as firmly as he could, he said, "Halt, who goes there?" "I don't mean no harm, I'm just wantin' some coffee, Billy Yank." In the dim light of the waning half-moon, Joseph could barely discern the outline of a slender soldier about the same size as he was. His body odor was pungent and sour, though not much worse than some of the men in his own regiment, including himself, who hadn't bathed in over a month. He couldn't see his face very clearly, but he could discern some moonlight bouncing off a peppery beard. His voice sounded like it belonged to an older man, but it was hard to be sure. Joseph was relieved to see that he had no musket, but he was still cautious because he knew the Rebs were fond of large knives, an instrument of death that would be hard to see in such faint light. Joseph was speechless. He was now face to face with the enemy, but he didn't know what to do. Some of his comrades had told tales of meeting gray-clad soldiers while on picket duty, but Joseph always found the idea of a personal encounter with the enemy to be surreal and far-fetched. Moments passed and he couldn't find a word to say.

"Looky here, Billy. Me and my pards, we's plum outta coffee. I know you blue-bellies git it in yer rations. Shurly ya can spare some, can't ya? I got a nice plug o' bakker here. I'll give ya the whole thing fer jest one scoopful o' coffee." There was a brief pause until words finally came to Joseph's mouth. "Should I be talking to you? This doesn't seem right. Besides, I don't even smoke!" "Billy," came the gray man's response, "That don't make no difference. Ya kin chew it if you want to. Here, try some!" "Uh, no thanks," came Joseph's sheepish reply. "Well, I know ya got pards that smoke, don't ya? Ya probably can find some that'll chew it, too. Fer Heaven's sakes, son, just give me some coffee and I'll be on my way." Joseph slowly undid his haversack, reached in and pulled out a small muslin pouch of ground coffee. Fortunately, he hadn't yet traded it off for something he found more valuable. In this respect, Joseph was quite the oddball in his regiment. He just didn't like the taste of coffee and he didn't enjoy drinking anything that was scalding hot. The nameless Confederate handed over the tobacco plug with one hand and took the coffee pouch with the other. He quickly loosened the string and then deeply inhaled the aroma of the contents. "Ahhh, Billy, may God bless your soul! I'll remember this on Judgment Day! I'll put in a special word fer ya with Jesus. Say where 'bouts ya from, Yank? It's good to know y'all ain't all bad." "Pennsylvania . . . Dauphin County, Pennsylvania." Joseph was feeling more at ease now with this enemy stranger. "Where are you from?" "Missoura, I growed up in Missoura, at least till my maw and paw got the fever. I was jest 12, so my big brother took me here to Virginny to live with Aunt Belle. Her home ain't more than 50 miles from here. That was nigh on 30 years back, so I feel like Virginny's my home now. I sure wish I was at Aunt Belle's house tonight. She done me right, she sho' did. She's still livin'. If I kin make it through the war, I'll be goin' home to see her jest as fast as these two legs'll carry me. If'n I don't make it, I know I'll be seein' her in Heaven. She had to be a saint to put up with all I done."

"Missouri? You grew up in Missouri? Did you know my cousin, Daniel, Daniel Seal?" Joseph knew right after he spoke those words how stupid they must have sounded. A chuckle came from the Reb's throat. "Well, Billy, Missoura's a perty big place. I never met more'n half the folks that live there. I jest don't remember no Daniel Seal, but then he mighta been my neighbor jest 20 miles down the road. Did yer cousin go blue or gray?" "Gray," was Joseph's reply, "He joined the Confederate Army. He sent me a letter." "Well then, he must be a real speshul cousin. With kinfolk like that, I think I might get to likin' you, Billy. I better git goin' before I git to likin' ya too much. I'd see ya in hell, but I already been there and I git the feelin' that ain't where yer goin'. Let's jest plan on some more chattin' together in Heaven someday, okay Billy Yank?" The gray-clad trader, preacher, and conversationalist turned and headed back toward the woods. When he had taken about 12 paces, he stopped, turned to face Joseph and said, "I'll remember this, I sho' will. I sho' do thank ya Billy!" "It's Joseph, Joseph Seiders," came the reply from the young "Billy Yank." "Well Joseph, I'll think of ya the next time I take a swig o' cider, if'n I ever get one agin. Good night!"

In an instant he was gone. Silence returned to Joseph's outpost. Did this really happen? Should he tell his comrades the next day? There was plenty to think about and he had no trouble staying awake for the 2 hours that remained of his picket duty. Most of his thoughts concerned the tobacco plug. Should he toss it in the woods or hang on to it as barter? If he chose the latter, he knew he'd have to do some explaining.

Chapter Seven - A Letter From Home

On the last day of June in 1863, news reached the camp that Confederates had invaded Pennsylvania. On July 3rd, they could actually hear cannon fire from the Battle of Gettysburg. The Seiders boys had no idea of the carnage that had taken place, but they feared they'd soon be involved in the fight. Neither were they aware of what had happened to cousin Daniel in faraway Vicksburg and that he'd be a prisoner of the men in blue the very next day.

Near the end of July, the Seiders brothers got a letter from their father, Henry. Joseph was thirsty for news from home and he eagerly read it to both of his brothers. The letter was written in German just like the letters the brothers sent home in reply. They were comfortable with both languages, though they spoke English with their fighting comrades almost exclusively. His father wrote them of how spring planting was especially slow this year without the assistance of Joseph, Israel, and William. The Seiders family made do with some part-time hired help. Joseph's father did the bulk of the work, however. The Lord provided some fine weather and the corn was doing well. Most of it was over knee-high. By the third paragraph, there was some bad news. "I regret to inform you boys that Samuel died on April 1st. He hadn't been doing too well much of the winter and his appetite just dropped off to nearly nothing. He lay down one night and the next morning he was gone." Joseph stopped his reading. "Joseph, you ain't gonna cry, are ya?" William asked. No, he wouldn't cry, though he and Samuel went back a long time. Joseph was just 7 the first time he plowed behind him. It was a great moment and he'd never forget the praise of his father after he successfully came to the end of the row. He had a special attachment to that mule and now he'd never see him again. At this point he could handle the loss of a mule if he knew for certain he'd see his father and mother at least one more time. He'd always taken them for granted. In fact, he took lots of blessings for granted, but he vowed to himself it wouldn't be that way anymore.

"Come on, Joseph, get back to reading!" Israel barked impatiently. A paragraph assured the boys that both their parents were in good health. Their neighbor, Mrs. Knouff was missing her 46 year-old husband terribly while he was serving with the 107th Pennsylvania. She hadn't heard from him in several months and specifically asked Joseph and his brothers to be on the lookout for him. Well, that wouldn't be easy. It was nearly impossible to know where any other Pennsylvania Regiments were located, let alone find a particular soldier.

Joseph read on. The last paragraph crashed with a hollow thud in the pit of Joseph's stomach. "Mama got a letter from her sister in Missouri. She was sad to report that cousin Daniel had lost his right eye at Vicksburg." The thought was sickening to the young man in blue. He stopped reading, dropped the letter, and ran off to be alone.

The same eye he had struck fourteen years earlier had now been struck a much more savage blow spewed out by Union cannon. Unfortunately, he had already witnessed the gruesome reality of a soldier with his eye shot out, but the mental picture of his wounded cousin was even more difficult to deal with. How innocent it seemed watching a tiny amount of blood flow from their little boy fingers on the memorable 1850 summer day they became "blood brothers." What a stark contrast to the blood Joseph had too often seen oozing from dead and wounded men.

He struggled with the senselessness of the whole situation. A soldier from his own Union Army, though on a field of battle that seemed as distant as the moon itself, had done the cruel deed. But then, what if the 172nd had been sent to Mississippi, and what if it had been Joseph himself that pulled the cannon lanyard? The thought was sickening. He wished he could travel back to his childhood and undo the errant punch that had blackened Daniel's eye. He wished he could be standing beside the blue artillerymen in Mississippi to kick the barrel of his artillery piece just in time to send the disfiguring shell fragments safely off course. "Dear God," he prayed, "why, oh why did this have to happen?" As so many times before when Joseph felt distressed, he instinctively reached for the little New Testament in his haversack. Leafing aimlessly through the pages, in short order he arrived at the verse he long ago had underlined in the eighth chapter of Romans. "*All things work together for good to them that love the Lord and are called according to his purpose.*" He felt somewhat comforted. Maybe now, Daniel would be going home. That was it! Daniel wouldn't be much of a soldier half-blind. The Confederacy would send him home to be with his mother and older sisters. Well, maybe they'd assign him some menial task like rolling cartridges, but surely he'd go home first and live out the rest of the war safe from enemy weapons. Joseph felt much better. He started making plans for their reunion.

The sharp sound of a bugle snapped Joseph out of his reverie. It was time to fall in and be on the march again. He quickly put back his testament then took a quick glance at the small portrait of his parents and the carte-de-visite of Daniel in uniform. The former was a treasure his mother had given him on the day he left home back in October. The latter brought some teasing from a few of his comrades about carrying around a Reb's picture. He wasn't the only one who had Confederate kin and he simply tried to be discreet about looking at the picture. Each time he did, he prayed for Daniel's safety. Were his prayers for naught? He didn't think so. Daniel was still among the living and even if he were to die, Joseph truly believed God knew best about everything, no matter how insane things might seem. Someday, he'd understand all of it. He reminded himself of I Corinthians 13:12, a verse he'd committed to memory several years earlier. "*For now we see through a glass, darkly; but then face to face: now I know in part; but then shall I know even as also I am known.*"

A quick swallow of water from his nearly empty canteen and Joseph fell in place on the front rank between his brothers Israel and William. "Attention Comp'ny! Take arms!" came the command and all the men retrieved their muskets from the stacks. "Shoul-derrr, arms!"

The entire company mechanically brought their weapons to their right shoulders with synchronized precision. "Right face!" A quick turn and he was facing southward down the road with William on his right side and Israel in front of him. "Forwaaard march!" and they were on the move again. The welcome sound of the drum beats kept their feet in step. The merciless dust again rose up and they marched in pursuit of the Confederate Army. Skirmishers had been sent out over the past few days and contact had been made with the enemy. He had nervously fired a few shots at some small bands of retreating Confederates, but he had yet to "see the elephant," as the veterans would say. Though Joseph felt he was well prepared for his first battle, he had a gnawing fear that he might run, no matter how brave he convinced himself he was.

Chapter Eight - The Brothers Return

The day to "see the elephant" never came as the Confederates escaped across the Potomac and the term of enlistment for the 172nd Drafted Militia expired. They were all mustered out on August 1, 1863. For nine months, Joseph had been a soldier without a major fight. He knew that his cousin Daniel so far away did not have the same sort of luxury. From what his Aunt Catharine had told his mother, Daniel had been involved in serious battles almost continually since first entering the Confederate service. How Joseph wished the war was over and he could travel to Missouri to see him.

The train ride home was not quite as thrilling as the ride eight months earlier; in fact he slept most of the way. The hike back home from Harrisburg was on a hot and muggy day, but what a joyous reunion was waiting for Joseph and his brothers when they reached Powell's Valley and the farm! Tears of joy streamed down his mother's face as she ran from the porch to greet them. She was holding little Mary as Israel locked both in a tight embrace. Mary had grown considerably and cried tears of fear not recognizing any of these three blue-coated strangers. Theirs were tears of joy. Henry Seiders tried to look stern as he said, "Now that you boys are through playing soldier, maybe we can get some work done around here!" All three got a bear hug from him and Joseph couldn't help but notice a few tears on his face, something he'd never seen before. Displays of affection from the Seiders patriarch had been very rare once the boys reached their teen years.

Later that day, they feasted on a wonderful supper. After a steady diet of hard tack and salt pork, a meal prepared by his mother never tasted better. What a joy to be with the family again, just reveling in the sound of their parents' voices and the delightful conversations from 2 year-old Mary who'd quickly become reacquainted with her father and uncles. That night Joseph's brothers went to bed first, leaving him alone on the porch with his father.

"Son," said his father, "I can't tell you how thankful we are that you boys are home. Your ma and I prayed for you every night. God kept watch over each of you." "Thanks, Pa. I know you did and I'm thankful, too. I've done a lot of praying these past nine months. Pa ... are you ... well, I mean, does it bother you that we didn't get in a big fight? We weren't near as brave as you and ma seem to think we were."

"Joseph, now that's a strange question. I'm mighty proud of all of you boys, but being a soldier isn't the important thing. You could have sat out this whole thing and I'd still be proud as long as you're always a soldier for the Lord. We both know the war's far from over and I'm afraid you may still get the chance to prove how brave you are." Joseph noticed a slight quivering in his father's chin. "Lord, I pray you don't, I pray you.... Well, I think....Son it's late, we both need to get to bed. Tomorrow we can all thank God in his house for bringing you back safely." After nearly a year's absence, Joseph's feather bed felt heavenly. The nights of sleeping on the hard ground faded quickly from his thoughts. Silently he thanked God for his reunion with the luxuries of home. In minutes he was in a deep sleep. After the most restful night he'd had since leaving home, the first light of dawn entered through his bedroom window. He was dreaming of the summer of 1850. His deceased grandmother walked into the room and kissed him on the forehead. She told him his little cousin Daniel was waiting for him outside. In an instant he was chasing after him, calling him by name, but Daniel was laughing and running toward the creek. Joseph's legs seemed locked in slow motion. He just couldn't catch up with his cousin and he was awakened by his own voice calling Daniel's name. The dream seemed so real it was hard for Joseph to believe 13 years had elapsed since he and his cousin were immersed in that magical summer.

The smells of breakfast entered his nostrils and what a magnificent feast it was! Breakfast in camp was never like this! Joseph was truly blessed beyond measure. In church that morning, another great reunion took place. His mother insisted that Joseph and his brothers wear their uniforms and there were hugs and kisses from dozens of women, some relatives and other family friends. Interspersed were numerous firm handshakes and encouraging words from the men. In his thick German accent, the pastor read from the fifth chapter of Ephesians. He preached on thankfulness, which seemed quite appropriate for this blessed day, though his mind wandered back to the news he received about Daniel in early July. He prayed for God's healing hand to be upon him and tried to concentrate on the sermon and the joy of being home. Feelings of guilt attacked him as he thought of the thousands of wounded soldiers on both sides suffering far from home. Leaving the church, he caught a glimpse of his second cousin, Sarah Enders. She was only 16, five years younger than Joseph, but she'd blossomed into a lovely young woman. Her beautiful dark brown hair was tucked perfectly beneath a stylish hat and he decided her green dress with black trim could never be equally pretty on any other girl. She smiled and waved goodbye. They'd known each other since childhood from numerous family reunions at nearby farms and she had once actually fallen asleep in his lap when she was about 4 or 5. Her mother thought it was a precious moment, but Joseph's brothers teased him about it mercilessly for a week. Now that she'd grown up, it occurred to him that she was the picture of all things pure and good, directly opposite from much of what he'd seen in his army service.

The days passed quickly and soon it was harvest time. Joseph was happy to be back in the fields, especially since the weather was mostly beautiful. Maybe because he'd seen battlefield casualties, or maybe he was just thankful to have survived his military service, but this fall, he was much more keenly aware of the magnificent colors of the leaves. How could he have taken for granted the fiery, orange foliage of the stately old maples scattered throughout Powell's Valley? How could he have neglected to ever thank God for the sight of golden morning sunlight bathing the reds, greens, and yellows painted on the ridges that cradled the place of his birth? Work was a blessing. How much more enjoyable it was to be out in the fields with the warm sun on his back and his nostrils filled with all the wonderful smells of the farm! How blessed he was to work for his father and no longer be under the thumb of his commanding officers. The freedom was magnificent! The work was hard, but it gave Joseph such a wonderful sense of purpose. His mind would often wander with reckless abandon. What if each ear of corn he pulled was a bar of gold? In no time at all he'd have riches beyond measure. But then he knew he already had riches. Each ear was valuable. After all, you couldn't eat a bar of gold. Besides, if you did have huge quantities of gold, you'd be constantly worried about thieves taking it away from you. What if the mule he was leading with a sled piled high with fodder was suddenly transformed into a fine team of horses with gilded bridles and an ornate chariot rolling behind? He'd be the driver, a Roman official in charge of everything he could see. No, thanks. Joseph was happier with the mule. Why hadn't he been as content with farm life before he was drafted? Even shoveling manure was a blessing here at home surrounded by the love of his kin!

God had richly blessed all the Seiders' crops that year, and Joseph wasn't the only one thankful for it. As the family gathered for every meal that fall, the men took turns blessing the food. Without fail, thanks were always given for the abundant harvest. The nation was in the midst of a war and all the Seiders knew such blessings were not to be taken for granted. As it was written in James 1:17, *"Every good and perfect gift is from above, coming down from the Father of the heavenly lights, who does not change like shifting shadows."*

On several Sundays, Joseph was invited to have dinner with Sarah's parents after church. He always felt at ease with her family and they with him. It was delightful to walk with Sarah to the house, since their buggy wouldn't accommodate an extra rider and the distance was under a mile. He loved to just hear her voice and look at her smile, especially since she hadn't been smiling much after the passing of her brother on August 31st. She still was grieving over his loss, even though nearly two months had passed. Joseph Enders was nearly the same age as his second cousin, Joseph Seiders, and he'd also served in the 172nd Drafted Militia. By the time of their mustering out, he'd been promoted to sergeant. About two weeks after returning home, he became ill with a mysterious malady. The doctor couldn't say what it was and none of his remedies were successful. It rained the day of the funeral, and Sarah seemed to weep more than her parents. He was buried with military honors and the three Seiders brothers wore their uniforms out of respect for their former comrade and cousin.

Joseph and Sarah's Sunday walks were building a bond between the cousins. Joseph was beginning to picture a future with Sarah as his wife. By Christmas, he was debating in his mind about asking her to marry him. His brothers were starting to tease him about her and his parents had started asking questions. He had no doubt in his own mind that he loved her, but he was hesitant. His brother, Israel, had married on their trip to Missouri and his wife died in childbirth. Frankly, he couldn't comprehend how Israel could have survived such a tragedy. Joseph kept reminding himself that Sarah was his second cousin, his own flesh and blood, he just couldn't marry her and he'd have to find someone else. At this point, they'd never kissed each other but after church let out on Christmas Eve, as they were about to leave for their respective homes, he hugged her, looked deep in her eyes, and said, "Good night, Sarah." He turned quickly and walked home, the moonlit snow lighting his path. Now he'd done it! From that point on he couldn't keep her out of his mind. Conflicting thoughts were battling within his head from that point forward. Oh how magnificent was that short embrace! He desperately wanted to do it again, but he couldn't. What would he say to her now after being so foolishly impulsive? He saw her again a week later after the Enders family invited him to supper in their home on New Year's Eve. Sarah looked more beautiful than ever and he felt very awkward around her after his rashness a week earlier. Around the table, most of the conversation centered on the war and speculation on how it might end. As dessert was served, Sarah's father spoke his mind. "This war has continued far longer that I ever would have thought. Too many people have died, too many from our own county, some of them our own flesh and blood. I know our son would be with us tonight if this awful thing hadn't started. Perhaps it's the wrath of God being poured out for the sins of our country, perhaps not. I just pray it will all end soon. Joseph, don't you have a cousin on the other side?" "Yes sir, my first cousin, Daniel Seal. He's the son of my mother's sister. I met him when we were children and I saw him again two years ago when my brother and I went out to Missouri. He lost his right eye at Vicksburg. I really want to see him again when it's all over." "I hope you can," was Mr. Enders' reply. "I think we have a few other kin on the enemy side, but I just can't consider them the enemy. Wars aren't supposed to be with your own relatives, are they?" Joseph dabbed his lips with his napkin. "No sir, no they shouldn't be." What an understatement! If only he knew how much the thought of his one-eyed cousin was haunting him. Where was he tonight? Was he warm? Was he, too, in someone's comfortable home, eating a New Year's Eve dinner, or was he shivering and coughing in some cold, winter encampment? He looked at Sarah. Her eyes were about to well up with tears after her father's speech. Joseph knew he better make his exit. "Mr. Enders. . . I certainly can't thank you and your wonderful wife enough for this fine meal tonight. I can't thank you enough for all the kindness you've shown me since I came home. I'm so sorry this has been a year of tragedy for you, and I pray that 1864 will be far better. I wish I could stay longer, but I told my folks I'd be home before it got late, so I, I guess I better be going." Sarah's mother stood up. "It's been so good to have you with us, won't you please take some of my cake home to your parents?"

"Why yes, thank you, Mrs. Enders," said Joseph as he arose from the table. As he stepped out onto the front porch, Sarah and her mother stepped out with him. He fidgeted for a moment with the cake in his hand. The night was well below freezing and he wished he didn't have to leave. "Thanks once again, Mrs. Enders." He looked at Sarah's lovely face, illuminated by a lantern on the front porch. If her mother wasn't standing next to her, surely he'd wrap his arms around her a second time. "Sarah, I .... I wish you a very Happy New Year. Goodnight." With that he turned, walked down the steps and headed home.

Chapter Nine - Second Departure

Winter was coming to a close and the day came when the three brothers would re-enlist. Their father protested the whole idea, what with all the spring planting close at hand, but he knew they had to go, out of a sense of duty. Too many lives had already been lost and most folks in the area felt that the war needed to be finished, lest the deaths of their loved ones over the past three years be in vain. There was a sense of urgency now, a sense that if there wasn't one final effort, the war would be lost into one horrible, senseless slaughter.

Joseph gave Sarah the news after church on his last Sunday before leaving. She didn't take it well at all. Her chin quivered and she did all she could to hold back her tears. "Joseph, don't. Please, don't do it! You were drafted once and you've already given nearly a year's service to your country. You don't have to go twice. No one will think less of you if you stay. If we have a future together, please, please don't take a risk like this. Let your brothers go and you can help your father with the farming. It'll be planting time before you know it! Please, please Joseph, don't go, don't ...." At this point she started sobbing. Joseph wrapped his arms around her and felt her warm tears against his cheek. For a few moments he was quiet, then he broke his silence. "Sarah, I must. I simply have to do it. I can't let my brothers leave without me and I know I'd consider myself a coward if I stay." "But Joseph," she cried, "you'll never be a coward in my eyes. Never! Isn't that all that matters?" "It matters a great deal to me," Joseph whispered, "but I must do what I have to do. I love you Sarah, I love you like I've never loved anyone else before. If God wills that I come back alive, I promise I'll ask you to marry me and we'll never be apart, never again. Besides, there'll be bounty money for re-enlisting, so that will help us start our life together." "What good would that money be if you don't come back? Just what if you don't come back," she sobbed, "What then? How could I go on living?" Joseph felt a lump in his throat. He couldn't speak, so he just looked in her eyes. There was no longer any doubt now.

Sarah's love for him was as strong as his love for her. She threw her arms around him and her warm tears touched his cheek. For her petite size, the embrace was exceptionally strong. "Come back, Joseph, be sure to come back, I pray you'll just come back." With these words she released him and ran toward her house. Joseph felt sick to his stomach. Though for an instant he thought he might follow her, he stood still until she was out of sight. He turned and slowly walked home with a thousand thoughts racing through his head.

Mary Seiders knew her boys would soon be leaving her again, though she made every effort not to think about it. One night she was terrified by a horrible nightmare. She dreamt she was wandering across a battlefield. As guns thundered in the distance, she searched among the bodies of blue and gray soldiers for her beloved sons. Turning over a lifeless soldier in blue, her breath stopped as she saw the face of her own Joseph. She awoke gasping for air with her heart racing. Tears drenched her pillow as she muffled her sobs so as not to wake her husband. Once she had calmed down enough to walk, she quietly slipped from her bed and went straight to Joseph's room. Tenderly, she placed her hand on her sleeping son's forehead. He stirred slightly and she stepped back. She carefully examined the faces of each of her sleeping sons, remembering how she'd often secretly watched them sleeping when they were toddlers. Dropping to her knees, she whispered a prayer thanking the Lord for the birth of each of them and begging for His protection for them through whatever conflict they might face.

It was less than a week after this dream that the boys were ready to return to the war. The day was sunny and exceptionally warm for March. Henry's handshake seemed firmer to Joseph this time. Was he imagining things or did Joseph see his father's eyes watering? This time, Mary couldn't hide her emotions. Tears streamed down her face as she hugged Israel, William, and Joseph in turn. Joseph felt another lump in his throat. Try as he might, he couldn't hide his emotions either. A single tear ran down his face. One more blurred look into his mother's eyes and he turned and ran to catch up with his brothers who were now twenty yards down the lane. He didn't look back as he did the first time. He knew if he did, he'd never get past the farm's gate.

Chapter Ten - Sarah's Visit

The monotony and deprivations of life at Camp Curtin were much easier the second time around for the Seiders boys. Their prayers and Bible study didn't draw nearly as much ridicule as they did in the fall of 1862. Most of the men had seen the results of war, even if they hadn't experienced the horrors firsthand. The sobering reality that death could snatch them away at any time softened many a callous heart. The brothers missed the comforts of home, yet they weren't quite as homesick this time, at least not William and Israel. Joseph was homesick in another way, homesick for the company of his new love, his second cousin, Sarah Enders.

The third Sunday after they left home, Joseph saw some familiar faces among the visitors. It was Sarah and her parents! Was this really happening? Could they have traveled all the way to Harrisburg just to see him? Sarah was wearing a beautiful green dress with a white lace collar. Wisps of her lovely brown hair peeked out from under her matching green bonnet.

A short two hours passed like minutes that beautiful afternoon. In a way Joseph hoped he could have been alone with Sarah, but the presence of her parents, George and Susannah Enders, was almost as pleasant as being with their daughter. The conversation mostly concerned news from home and the progress of the war, but Sarah's parents made Joseph feel at ease. It was apparent to Joseph that they thought highly of him and were genuinely concerned for his welfare. He was in their prayers as well as Sarah's.

All too soon, it was time for them to go. Joseph wished he could freeze this moment in time. He knew quite well he might never see Sarah again. She stood alone for a moment as her parents stepped into their carriage. Impulsively, he grabbed a brass button from his sack coat, the second one from the top, and tore it off. "Sarah, please, take this," he told her. Her chin quivered slightly. She silently looked into his eyes, gathered her thoughts, then spoke. "I promise I'll sew it back when you come home. I'll wear it around my neck until then. Take my handkerchief. Keep it with you as a reminder of me." Her gloved hand touched his right cheek and her lips gave a quick kiss to his left. She started to cry, quickly turned and ran toward the carriage. As they drove off, she took one more glance back at Joseph, before they disappeared from view.

Chapter Eleven - New Hope Church

Much of the month of May in 1864 was occupied with hundreds of miles of marching for Daniel Seal and his Missouri comrades. They crossed Alabama heading for Georgia with a welcome 60-mile train ride along the way. Daniel had been promoted to 2nd Lieutenant back in March. He felt it was not due to any particular military skill, but simply that too many officers had died or were incapacitated. The threat of Gen. William T. Sherman to Atlanta had brought Daniel and the Army of Tennessee to Georgia. With his 54,000 men, Gen. Joseph E. Johnston was doing the best he could to defend against the 100,000 blue-coated invaders. During the latter part of May, there was constant skirmishing with the enemy, punishing heat during the day, drenching rains at night, and a constant supply of lice, ticks, and flies. Thick woods and brush on hilly, muddy terrain made the army's movement difficult, but these were seasoned soldiers who were well accustomed to hardship. General Cockrell marched his Missouri Brigade to the vicinity of New Hope Church during the night of May 24th. The church was a humble log structure built by the Methodists. The Missourians formed a thin line in a single rank. Too many men had been lost for an additional rank or any men in reserve.

As the fighting intensified late in the afternoon of the 25th, Daniel couldn't help but think how under alternate circumstances, he'd be worshipping in the little church. His own family back in Missouri had been Methodists since before he was born. He was thankful for the regimental chaplain who held services every Sunday they weren't engaged in battle. Though not quite the same as the more comfortable church services of his boyhood, it was a joy to see the Spirit move among some of the most hardened of hearts. Daniel had prayed for some of the most hateful and blasphemous men in his company. Some were heavy drinkers and vile enough to make it hard for anyone to get along with them. When one in particular gave his heart to Jesus on

Easter Sunday in 1863, Daniel rejoiced as did many of his comrades. He had been known as "Bad Bill" to his fellow soldiers, but he was completely transformed that day and everyone knew it. Less than two months later, he was killed at Vicksburg. Daniel was certain that was one soul Satan had lost. In fact, though Satan must have taken delight in all the slaughter of the last three years, he was losing a lot more souls than just that of "Bad Bill." As the war progressed, many men came to realize they could die at any moment and spend eternity in either one of two places. Great revivals swept through the Confederate Army and thousands entered the Kingdom of Heaven who may not have done so had the war not come.

Like a carefully orchestrated concert, thunder grew progressively louder around New Hope Church as both a violent storm and enemy guns drew closer to Daniel and his comrades. The rain was drenching, but he'd been a military man for far more than a thousand days now. He'd experienced a great diversity of discomforts, he'd seen the horrors of war, and he was no longer a carefree, eight year-old boy catching frogs with his Pennsylvania cousin. He was a man of 22 years who had witnessed things some men might never see in 80 years of life. He was a Confederate soldier in a ragged uniform whose life could be snuffed out in an instant. The thought that this day might be his last briefly crossed his mind as it did in all the previous engagements. As the fighting grew hotter, Daniel became preoccupied with keeping his powder dry, loading his musket, and digging himself into the protection of the sticky, red Georgia clay. For several nights, his home was a deep, muddy trench with a shallow pool of water for a floor. Finally, Daniel's regiment was ordered to move again. Though the casualties had been light for the Missouri boys, Daniel was glad to leave the place that his blue-suited enemies had named the "Hell Hole."

It was good to be on the march once more, though the rain and the skirmishing continued. In early June, as the Confederates paused, Daniel headed off alone to take care of bodily functions. Soon he stumbled upon a wounded Union soldier in some thick forest undergrowth. He'd heard some faint groaning and followed the sound, expecting to find one of his own men. "Maybe I can find a surgeon," Daniel blurted to the dying soldier whose face was nearly white. "No need. I know I'm a goner." Shiny green flies buzzed around a large wound on his right shoulder. Though the man wasn't dead, a putrid smell of rotting flesh wafted from the wound and small maggots wiggled within it.

"Well, where ya from?" Daniel asked as calmly as he could. He felt he needed to make conversation, if for no other reason than to give a fellow human being some dignity in his last moments on earth.

"Pennsylvania."

Immediately, Daniel thought of Joseph. "My cousin lives there! Lives near Harrisburg. Do you live there, too?"

"Nope, I'm from out west . . . . near Pittsburgh." The wounded Yankee was gasping, fighting to utter each sentence. "Friend, write my Maw. Please, will ya do that for me? Take my haversack. Her name's on the letters she wrote me."

"Look, I'll just take a letter and leave the food with..."

The dying young man in blue interrupted, "No! Take it all. I won't be needin' food no more. Just ...just look at me, Brother. I know this is it." The lower part of his sack coat was caked with dried blood and a small trickle continued to flow to the ground. Maybe he'd been wounded the night before; maybe the night before that. The flies caressed his face as he spoke. "Friend, I can't even see no more. I can feel the blood...I can feel it spillin' outta me just like it spilled from Jesus' side. He's the one I'll see next and I ain't scared. I ain't..... scared. I ain't." The blue soldier spoke no more. A gurgling sound came out of his throat followed by a few sputtering coughs. In a few moments, a slight smile came to his face and his body became motionless. What a difference, Daniel thought, from the death he'd witnessed of the soldier at Big Black River just a little over one year ago. Daniel leaned forward and closed the Pennsylvanian's eyes that gazed up to Heaven. He was confident that's where he was. He carefully took the haversack from the now lifeless body, walked twenty paces further into the woods and finished what he'd originally set out to do. He'd been gone from his regiment a fairly good while, but nobody asked any questions. A large portion of the men were suffering from dysentery, and extended breaks for relief were nothing out of the ordinary.

That night, Daniel looked through contents of the haversack by the light of a smoky fire. All the firewood was soaked from the rains and the humidity and mosquitoes made for an unpleasant night. He felt like he was violating another man's home by going through his personal belongings, though he was thankful to find two soggy pieces of hardtack. Silently, he thanked the Lord for the blessing of some food and the knowledge that the man who provided it was now in the presence of Jesus. How totally strange that an enemy soldier had called him "Brother," yet he knew that the dying man was truly his brother in Christ. As he dined on the hardtack, he read one of the letters in the dim light of the camp fire. Though he knew he couldn't do it now, Daniel prayed that the Lord would somehow allow him to write to the dead soldier's mother. The opportunity arose one steamy afternoon two days later during a lull in the fighting. The sun was out and he was able to sufficiently dry two blank sheets of paper that he found in the haversack. Surely this was an act of God, since paper was extremely hard to come by for Confederate soldiers at this point in the war. Using a pencil that was also in the haversack, Daniel started to write:

Georgia

7 June, 1864

Dear Mrs. Wallace,

It is my sad duty to inform you of the passing of your son, Pvt. Isaac Wallace. He fell bravely from enemy fire near New Hope Church. I have seen men die before in this cruel war, but it pleases me to tell you that your son died with Jesus. I have every confadence he is with Him now. It is hard to considder Pvt. Wallace my enemy when I know we have the same Father in Heaven. I have a cosin in this war who is from Pennsylvania. If he dies or I die, know that we will meet your son in that fair land.

Your Obedient Servant,

2nd Lt. Daniel Seal

1st Missouri Cav.

At this point in the war, it was seriously doubtful the letter would make it past the enemy lines, but he fervently prayed that God would miraculously direct it to the dead Yankee's mother. It wasn't unheard of for the men in his regiment to send letters to the other side. Like Daniel, many of the men had brothers and cousins serving the Union. Many had families living in what was now Union territory. After writing to the far away mother who didn't even know as yet that she'd lost a son, Daniel decided he'd have time to write a letter to his cousin Joseph. The last letter he'd received from him had arrived just before the fighting began at New Hope Church. Joseph was in a new regiment now, the 187th Pennsylvania Infantry. Daniel poured his heart out through his short stub of a pencil, reread what he'd written, and sealed the letter in an envelope fashioned from the Pittsburgh soldier's last piece of paper. Again, he prayed that God would guide the letter safely to its intended destination. He then pulled his crumbling gum blanket over his shoulders and went to sleep with his back propped against a large, wet boulder.

On the 18th of June, the Missouri Brigade was on the move again as had been the case for weeks. Little did he know what was in store on this very day for his beloved first cousin, Joseph, 800 miles away. Neither did Daniel know what lay ahead as he and his fellow Missourians slogged through the wet Georgia clay on their way to Kennesaw Mountain.

Chapter Twelve - Moving Toward Petersburg

It was June 16, 1864. There was no more doubt about it, they were headed toward a fight. General Grant had the whole Army of the Potomac moving and on this beautiful morning in June, Joseph knew the 187th would be moving with them. Bugles were blowing, drums were beating, and orders were being barked. The entire 5th Corps was issued three day's rations. The 187th Regiment of nearly a thousand soldiers was being assembled in one long column of men, four abreast. The other regiments of the Corps were doing likewise. It was a grand sight, but a sobering one. How many of these thousands of blue-coated citizen soldiers would be gone just a week from now? How many would take up permanent residence in Heaven and how many in hell? The thought of dying wasn't terrifying to Joseph, he just didn't like the idea of the grief his family would have to experience. Neither did he like the idea of never again seeing Sarah's lovely, smiling face, at least never again in this earthly life. Why dwell on the negative? There was nothing to worry about, was there? Joseph had complete confidence as to where he'd spend eternity, not because of anything he'd done to deserve it, but solely because of the incomprehensible love of God who sacrificed his own Son for Joseph's transgressions. How could anyone refuse such a gracious and magnificent gift?

"Attention Battalion! Right Face! Forwarrrd, March!" Joseph's left foot moved forward mechanically just like 900-some other left feet. He was on the outside left, about in the middle of the 100 men in Company H. William was on his right and Israel directly in front. The early morning sun glinted off thousands of bayonets bobbing up and down like waves on a great sea. Multitudinous pairs of feet tramping in unison created a sound like a huge beast thundering over the earth, punctuated by the tinkling rhythm of tin cups and the accoutrements of each soldier as they marched through the countryside. He was struck by the serpentine motion of nearly a thousand parts all working together to form one huge creature crawling over the land. A beast so large would seem indestructible, but Joseph knew an enemy attack could cut it to pieces.

In a very short time, they came to a halt on the bank of the James River. While they waited for other regiments to be ferried across in transports hauled by a steam tugboat, the 187th was permitted to bath in the river. What a pure joy it was! The water was clear and clean, and only slightly cold. Joseph thanked the Lord for this wonderful blessing as the sweat and filth of the past month was washed away. Truly, only God could provide such a wonderful cleansing. After about ten minutes, it was time for the men to put their uniforms back on. To a man, they all filled their canteens with the clear water of the James. Soon they were on the far side of the river and the march resumed.

The weather had been hot and dry for days and great clouds of dust were kicked up by the thousands of marching soldiers. The relative coolness of the morning was soon gone. The temperature soared and the woolen sack coats that were such a comfort on cool days and nights became instruments of torture. Like all the rest of the men, Joseph's shirt was uncomfortably soaked under his blue uniform. Periodically, he could feel streams of sweat run down his back.

As the long march proceeded and the sun climbed higher, Joseph realized his canteen was becoming alarmingly light. He'd have to ease up on his water consumption, but that wouldn't be easy with the intensifying heat. Many of the men were muttering whispered complaints laced with some choice cuss words as the temperature rose. Some of the men were becoming noticeably irritable, while others marched on without complaint. Sweat was trickling down the small of Joseph's back when the First Sergeant hollered, "Carryyyy, arms!" A low voice from one of the privates replied, "Well just whaddya think I've been doin' all day long?" Joseph stifled a laugh. He was thankful for those that kept their sense of humor, no matter how uncomfortable the circumstances might be.

The incessant chorus of cicadas kept him ever mindful of the sweltering heat. He'd always associated some of the hottest days on the farm with the sound of these insects that spent the majority of their lives underground. Just the day before, Joseph had seen one crawling up a tree trunk while another was squeezing out of his old body through a long slit in his back. Though he was pale and nearly motionless, his newly acquired wings were clearly visible. Those whose bodies had been transformed couldn't stop singing about their newly acquired freedom from the dark and damp confinement of the soil. The thought served to remind him that things could be far worse. He was alive, he was breathing, and even if he was felled by a hurtling lead ball in the next minute, he had complete confidence that his eternity would be in Heaven and not hell. Even a young cicada's life would be joyful in comparison with eternity in hell, eternal separation from God's love. Joseph knew with certainty, someday he'd be like those cicadas. He'd be released from all the unpleasantries of this present world and he'd sing for joy upon his arrival in the next. For the first time in his life, he prayed a prayer of thanksgiving for insects.

Late in the day, he drank the last water from his canteen. His brother, Israel, had some left and shared a swallow. Most all of the men were now out of water. If only they could stand by the banks of the James once more! At sunset, a halt was sounded and the men hoped it meant the end of a long day of marching and perhaps the discovery of a source of water. Unfortunately, several more hours of marching into the night were to follow. Word was passed along that they wouldn't stop until water was reached. By the time the final halt was sounded, the 5th Corps had marched twenty-six long, weary miles. In the pale moonlight, they all stacked arms in a large field that would be bed for the night. Joseph and his brothers were excited at the prospect of filling their canteens. It was quite a disappointment to find the water would come from a stagnant swamp. In the dim light of a few lanterns, a green scum covered the surface. As the men brushed it aside, some could see tiny wiggling creatures that only a very few of them recognized as immature mosquitoes. Thankfully, Joseph still had the handkerchief that Sarah had given him on the wonderful day of her visit. He wrapped it tightly around the mouth of his canteen to filter the water as he filled it. His first swallow was nearly nauseating. It was lukewarm and had a bitter, repulsive flavor. His thirst was great and somehow he managed two more swallows before bedding down in the dry grass. Musketry and cannon fire could be heard in the distance. Before finally dozing off, Joseph thought this could very possibly be his last night on earth.

Very early the next morning, the gargantuan march began again. Joseph had slept fitfully during the night and his bowels were beginning to protest against the water he'd drank. He had been so parched, he just had to drink it, but upon seeing the swamp in the daylight, he wondered if he could have consumed any of its water had it not been shrouded in darkness. At least his officers had allowed the men to sleep. He'd heard tales of some regiments marching throughout entire nights. This day's march was basically a repeat of the previous day's experience, though sadly lacking the bath in the river. Many of the men had dumped out their canteens after the first taste of the horrible contents, but soon the stifling heat had them wishing they hadn't. The morning coffee wasn't much better, but the majority of soldiers were too habituated to it to go without. At least the boiling process killed the wiggling creatures that had been snatched from their swampland home. Joseph decided that morning that a canteen full of leftover swamp coffee would be better than his filtered water. Though he didn't like coffee, it helped mask the awful taste. As the day dragged on, he took occasional sips and shared some with men who'd poured out their canteens that morning. No water would be had until they reached their destination near Petersburg that afternoon.

Eventually, the day's grueling march came to a halt. The sounds of fierce fighting were now louder than ever. The 5th Corps was now in support of the 9th Corps that was already hotly engaged with the enemy. Joseph knew his first major engagement was close at hand. Both his brothers knew it and they didn't hesitate to verbalize their anxiety to him. At any moment, the order might come to form up for battle. While they waited, some of the men successfully dug for water. Though not as pure as the James River water, it was still a wonderful blessing in comparison with the previous night's swamp water. Joseph's bowels were now cramping severely from its effects. As he squatted in the woods for relief, he couldn't help notice the golden light of the setting sun bathing the beautiful green foliage of white oak, sweetgum, and Virginia pine trees. The Book of Revelation spoke of the holy city, the New Jerusalem made of pure gold. Maybe he'd be seeing it shortly. Suddenly, the regiment was called to formation. Joseph pulled up his pants as quickly as possible and ran to the spot where he and the others had stacked their arms. Orders were barked and Joseph responded like a machine, just as he'd done hundreds of times before in drill. "Arms port! Forwarrrd, March!" The line moved toward the enemy. Shells exploded to the front and rear, close but not too close for casualties.

No shots were fired by the 187th and they were ordered to fall back, accomplished in fine order, then held in reserve. The days were long at this time of year, but mercifully, darkness slowed the fighting down, almost to a complete halt. All the Seiders brothers silently thanked the Lord for their miraculous deliverance from the battlefield. Joseph knew it could have been much worse, but he and his brothers survived. He knew there would be more action the next day and he had an ominous feeling about it. Even when darkness arrived, none of the three brothers was quick to go to sleep. Though dog-tired from two days of marching, nervousness and cramping stomachs kept them awake. That night, Joseph whispered a prayer as he lay on his back staring at the night sky. "Dear Lord, I thank Thee for protecting me and my brothers from harm. I ask Thee to do the same tomorrow if it be Thy will. Please watch over my family at home. I miss them and I pray Thou will let me see them again. And please, Lord, please let me see Sarah again if it be Thy will. If I should die, I thank Thee for the price Jesus paid at Calvary so I can live forever in Heaven. If I die, please comfort Sarah and give her a godly husband. In Jesus' Name, Amen." The last request was difficult. If indeed he did die, he truly wanted God to give Sarah a godly husband, but the thought made him cry unseen in the darkness. He loved Sarah deeper than he'd ever loved anyone. If by some miracle he survived the war, he wanted to be Sarah's husband more than anything he'd ever wanted before.

Chapter Thirteen - June 18, 1864

Morning tiptoed in. Birds started to sing and gray light leaked into the darkness of the regiment's forest bedroom. It was June 18, 1864. Joseph had slept very little the night before. He dreamed for short periods and then awakened in a sweat. The dreams made no sense, just a collection of recent events and those from long ago, mixed together in a random fashion. The stomach cramps hadn't left him. The moon was nearly full, so his three trips to the latrines weren't as difficult had they been made in total darkness. Each time, he was joined by some of the same soldiers. On his last visit, one of them quipped, "Pard, it's good to see ya again, but maybe you ortn't a left. I spent the whole night here with my breeches down!" At the sound of reveille, the cramping wasn't quite as bad for Joseph. He quickly picked up his bedroll and donned his sack coat and accoutrements and soon he was standing in formation with the rest of Company H. His brother Israel was on his right, and his brother William behind him in the rear rank. Clouds had rolled in during the night and the air was hot, humid, and still. A hollow feeling had invaded his stomach, not so much from the lack of breakfast or the cramps from the bad water, but mostly from knowing this was *the* day. There was no longer any doubt. Today would be *the big one*, the biggest battle of his life. This would be the real thing, not some minor skirmish he was in over a year ago with the 172nd. While the roll was being called, Joseph heard the incessant crowing of someone's rooster at a nearby farm. He was reminded of Peter's denial of Jesus three times before the cock crowed. What would Joseph have done had he been in Peter's shoes? Surely he wouldn't have betrayed his Lord, just to save his own skin, or would he? What about today? Would he betray his country to save his own skin? As soon as the battle got hot and heavy, would he skedaddle straight to that rooster in the distance that couldn't keep quiet? No, he just couldn't, could he? Prayer seemed like the logical action now. That's what King David would have done before each of the many battles he was in. Joseph silently prayed earnestly for the Lord to empower him to be brave and strong during the fight that loomed ahead. He prayed for the safety of his brothers and himself as well as all the men in his company. The prayer continued even after the order was given to face right and begin marching. Prayers went up requesting comfort for his dear mother and father should he or his brothers be killed. Likewise, a prayer went up for the girl he'd grown to love and now missed so dearly. "Father, if it's in Thy will, please allow me to live so I might someday marry Sarah. If not, just give her comfort and strength and allow her to find the husband Thou would choose for her."

The regiment marched like a giant piece of machinery. Seven companies marched before his own Company H, each with nearly a hundred men. As the column climbed uphill and curved to the right, Joseph thought it resembled a slithering blue serpent. As they emerged from the shadows of great oaks, the early morning sun glinted off waves of bayonets. Once more, Joseph thought it resembled a single, giant creature. Was it a mechanical snake, crawling homeward to hell? "*And the great dragon was cast out, that old serpent, called the Devil, and Satan, which deceiveth the whole world.*" Surely Satan was part of this, this whole insanity of war. Maybe this would be the end of it, the end of the war, but he knew today would be the last day for hundreds, if not thousands of men. In any case, Joseph knew he couldn't dwell on the horror of it all. He reminded himself that his home was in Heaven. Should today be the day he'd go home, that old serpent could never torment him again.

The sound of artillery became louder as the robotic column moved onward. A shell burst to the right, showering dirt on Joseph and his brothers. At this moment he knew that today might very well be his last on earth. A nervous voice began to chirp off to his left. "This is it boys! The Rebs'll kill us all! They'll cut us into sausage! Look at all of 'em behind the breastworks! We haven't got a chance!" An angry sergeant hollered, "Quiet in the ranks! For God's sake, quiet in the ranks!" More shells exploded. They were getting way too close now.

Joseph could now see off in the distance an elaborate line of breastworks fashioned from logs and mud. Here and there along the line, a puff of white smoke would appear, followed shortly by a loud booming sound. He was to be part of an assault on this fortress, an assault that might very well end his life on earth.

A command suddenly invaded Joseph's ears. "On the right by file into line!" Instantly, the column of four men abreast was transformed into a wall of men two deep facing the enemy's breastworks. "Company, fire by file! Ready! Commence firing!" In military precision, the musket fire of each man and his file partner rapidly traveled down the line. William shouted, "Fire!," and the two brothers simultaneously pulled their triggers. Immediately, Joseph began the reloading process. His hands were shaking as he poured the black powder down the barrel and stuffed the cartridge in the muzzle. He pulled his rammer and forced the cartridge home as he'd done so many times before. He pulled a percussion cap from his pouch but his fingers trembled too much to place it on the musket's nipple and it dropped to the ground. The noise of battle was now louder than anything he'd previously experienced. The brass cap was on the ground and he started to kneel to pick it up. He stopped himself halfway, straightened up and reached in his cap pouch for another. Just when he thought the sound level could grow no louder, massive artillery fire opened up from the Confederate works. To his right, he heard horrible screams as a hole was torn in the lines. Officers were screaming and cursing at the top of their lungs. Bugle calls could be heard, but all was mass confusion now. The line began to move forward and Joseph moved with them. His legs were shaky and he felt as if his lifeblood had taken on a mind of its own, coursing through all the wrong places so he had to consciously tell his body to move. Warm blood suddenly splattered his ear. The man to his left had been hit in the neck. His right arm clutched Joseph's side as he collapsed on the dirt. The regiment continued to advance as up and down the line men randomly dropped to the ground.

As the huge force continued to move forward and the sounds of battle grew ever louder, Joseph's mind took him back to a Sunday in 1850. He was standing in church next to his cousin Daniel. They were sharing a hymnal singing Martin Luther's "Mighty Fortress" in German. *"A mighty fortress is our God, a bulwark never failing."* Another shell crashed way too close, taking out two men not far from his left. *"The body they may kill: God's truth abideth still, His kingdom is forever."* Reality returned. Explosions were everywhere. Acrid smoke filled his nostrils and clouded his vision. The noises were deafening. Joseph's lips sent out a prayer that no one else could hear. "Dear God, please protect us, spare us if it's within Thy will, in Jesus' name." The smoke, the deafening roar of battle, the screams of the wounded and dying, all of it was totally out of control. He could feel the earth shake beneath his feet. Joseph knew his time on earth could be over in just seconds. Horrible, filthy curse words were spewing out of the mouths of soldiers up and down the line. A battle had now begun to rage in his brain as well. A voice was now shouting, "Run, run, save your hide, run you fool! Turn around and run. Get out of here! Get out now while you still can!" He couldn't! He knew it was the crafty old serpent talking. He wouldn't listen. How could he face his family, how could he face Sarah if he survived this engagement by running? No, he had to move forward, he just couldn't turn tail and run. He was David facing Goliath and he was depending on God for deliverance. The roar of battle raged on. How long had he been in this fight? Was it two hours? Was it two minutes? Time had left the earth. Clocks no longer existed, or did they? Surely this couldn't go on forever, could it? Could this be hell? Was he trapped here forever? Just then, a hand grabbed his ankle. It belonged to a wounded soldier and Joseph stumbled to his knees. At that very moment, a piece of shrapnel struck his right shoulder. Joseph felt no pain, but the deafening sound of war became suddenly quiet. His eyes were open but the gruesome picture before him turned solid white. He felt as if his blood had totally deserted him. For a short moment, he stayed upright on both knees, but his body was no longer his to control. Joseph fell face forward in the dirt.

The bouncing of an ambulance awakened Joseph. How long had he been out? The sun was setting, so it had to have been hours. Even though the day was hot, he was cold from the loss of blood. Pain wracked his right shoulder as the ambulance rattled and jostled his body. He placed his hand on his wound. His sack coat had a gaping hole in it, surrounded by shredded strips of crimson wool. He glanced at his hand, now covered with blood. The sight reminded him of his first witness of a hog butchering. Sweat covered his face, but he was shivering. Surely this horrible wound was mortal. Joseph stared at the ambulance canopy and saw reddish brown splatter marks. Was it blood? How did it ever get up there? How many people had died riding in this wagon? How many went from here to Heaven? How many didn't? He prayed without speaking. Soon he'd be entering Heaven's gates. The pain in his shoulder would leave. All this insanity would be gone forever. He'd be seeing his grandparents, Sarah's brother, Joseph Enders, and all his comrades who preceded him. He thanked God for his many blessings, but regretted not being able to see his parents and Sarah one last time. In a voice drowned by the sound of the creaking ambulance wheels, Joseph murmured, "Not my will, but Thine." He passed out.

Chapter Fourteen - Kennesaw Mountain

General Joe Johnston was moving his Army of Tennessee like a chess piece. After New Hope Church, his men would march to places named Dallas, Pickett's Mill, Brushy Mountain, Gilgal Church, Lost Mountain, Pine Mountain, and Mud Creek before reaching Kennesaw Mountain in the deadly chess game with General William T. Sherman. On the morning of June 18, 1864, Daniel was entrenched at Latimer's Farm along with the rest of the Missouri Brigade under the command of General Cockrell. The Yankees attacked with fierce artillery fire during a severe thunderstorm. The Missouri boys were driven back. Daniel had no idea that while he was enduring this miserable pandemonium, his beloved cousin Joseph had been wounded by an artillery fragment at Petersburg. Much of the next day was spent digging trenches and dodging Yankee artillery fire. It was hot, muddy and muggy, but few complaints were heard. That night around a smoky camp fire, Daniel surveyed his comrades of the past two years. Most were good men who trusted the Lord. Some were non-believers who didn't want to hear "religious talk." Many who were once part of his regiment were absent, their lives snuffed out in past battles. There was little conversation that night, but Daniel spoke with his close friend, Alfred Everett. Daniel was somewhat embarrassed that Alfred hadn't been the one promoted to 2nd Lieutenant back in March. Daniel was six years younger and he felt uncomfortable being superior in rank to an elder. This didn't affect their friendship, however. Daniel said, "Should anything happen to me, you'll write my ma, won't ya?" "Sure," came Alfred's reply. "Ya know I would, Daniel, ya know I would. But hey, you'll do the same for me if ya have ta, won't ya?" Somehow, Daniel felt he'd go first. For him the war had gone past the point of insanity. The muddy, miserable existence just couldn't go on much longer. The horrors he'd seen were too gruesome to ever leave him. He sat at the base of a pine tree, prayed for his family, including his Pennsylvania cousin, then started a conversation with God about why things had to be the way they were. He was still in prayer when he fell asleep.

Daniel was awakened by the sound of an artillery shell, just as the first morning light appeared. He hurried back to the safety of the trenches and was soon joined by a good number of his comrades. His friend, Sgt. Everett was beside him. Both their muskets had fresh rust on the barrels from the dampness of the night, so they set about rubbing it off as best they could with a shared, tattered rag. "Treasures in Heaven," said Daniel. "Huh?" was Alfred's only reply. "Remember, Jesus said don't lay up treasures on earth where moth and rust corrupt." "Well, we got plenty o' rust," said Alfred, "maybe not a whole lotta moths, but the dang skeeters'll do!" Daniel looked toward the location of the enemy artillery. "Maybe so, but we both got treasures in Heaven."

Artillery fire became more intense. Then came a screaming whistle and other soldiers around them witnessed a horrible sight. In an instant, a small projectile from a cannon shell found its mark in Daniel's head. His young life was snuffed out at age 22 in a senseless war that had already snuffed out thousands of others. Nothing could be done; all the men knew the damage was mortal. Sgt. Everett wept openly as did others in the regiment who'd grown to love this young man who had served his Lord so faithfully.

Who knows what Daniel might have done had he survived, married and had a family. Who knows how much more service he could have rendered as a soldier for the Lord. Daniel's mother would be heart-broken, as would his siblings and Pennsylvania cousins. It could have been just one more death among countless others. It could have been completely forgotten had a written record not been made. His earthly trials were over, but most importantly, Daniel's name was recorded in the Lamb's Book of Life and He who is all-knowing told Daniel, "Well done, good and faithful servant." Daniel was home!

Chapter Fifteen - Return to Powell's Valley

The time at camp in Philadelphia seemed to go on forever. Menial tasks that seemed to have little purpose filled the days of the Seiders boys. Young officers who'd never been in battle morphed into little Napoleons, searching for the slightest infraction of military rules to exert their authority and humiliate their underlings. A few of the veteran soldiers couldn't tolerate it and wound up with court-martials when they forcefully challenged the little dictators. A hunger for home permeated the camp and when the day finally arrived for mustering out, many of the veterans wept for joy. When Joseph boarded the train for Harrisburg, his mind went back to the thrill of his first train ride. He knew he was greatly blessed to be headed home, alive, with nothing missing except maybe his former innocence of the horrors of war. In a period of just three years, he'd witnessed far too much of the results of sin's entry into the world. Only by God's grace had he survived what could have been a mortal shell wound. It was many months before he rejoined his regiment, but mercifully, they had been sent to Philadelphia, far from the horrors of battle. Though still deprived of many civilian comforts, the monotony of camp life was bearable knowing the war was nearing an end.

Finally, they were going home. Joseph and his brothers were all veteran soldiers now and also veteran riders of the rails. Joseph even had a battle scar that would always be a reminder of the horrors of war. Many a time he would stare at it and think of the scars on the hands, feet and side of Jesus. As the train chuffed toward Harrisburg, little did he know he'd have children and grandchildren who'd stare at the scar and he'd use it to teach them about the scars of a Savior.

He enjoyed watching the beautiful Pennsylvania farmland pass by his window, but fitful sleep with jumbled, nightmarish dreams filled most of the hours back to Harrisburg. They train arrived well after dark, so the three brothers slept on the ground and began the final leg of their journey home early the next morning. Ascending Peter's

Mountain seemed more demanding than their previous climbs. The boys spoke little, each lost in thoughts of what they'd experienced in the war and what might lay ahead in peace-time. Upon reaching the crest, their mood changed much for the better with their first glimpse of Powell's Valley. That magnificent patchwork of farms, fields, and forests was their home and always would be. They'd made a visit to hell and now they were about to return home to the place closest to Heaven, until their earthly lives were over. The descent down the mountain went quickly and by late afternoon, they'd reached the lane that lead to their boyhood home. Joseph felt a lump well up in his throat. What a blessing it was to see a split-rail fence without lifeless bodies of soldiers beside it. What a blessing it was to hear only the sounds of crickets and birds rather than muskets and artillery. What joy filled his nostrils thanks to the wonderful smells of nature and the farm rather than black powder smoke and decaying human flesh. By the time he could see the front porch, tears streamed down his cheeks. The dogs were first to greet the brothers and their barking alerted Mary and Henry. The reunion took place just five yards from the porch steps. Joseph was first to embrace the mother who'd born all three. Their father looked considerably older than the mere year and a half ago since they last left him, but his bear-hug for Israel was youthful. William was next in their mother's arms and soon the whole family had been reacquainted. Israel's daughter Mary had grown about six inches and this time, she was thrilled to see her dad. Tears of joy flowed freely and shortly they were sitting on the front porch looking out over God's bountiful blessings while Mary busied herself in the kitchen. Few meals would be as memorable to the Seiders boys as the supper they enjoyed as the sun set over Powell's Valley. It began with a lengthy blessing by the Seiders patriarch and went on for more than two hours. There were mashed potatoes, gravy, roast beef, peas, carrots, corn, and much conversation to catch up on all that had occurred during the boys' absence. It was the summer of 1865 and for Joseph, Israel, and

William Seiders, the Civil War was over. Miles away in Missouri, their Aunt Catharine was still mourning the loss of her youngest son over a year earlier. Life went on, but the war's consequences were felt for generations.

Epilogue

On November 29, 1866, Joseph married his second cousin, Sarah Ellen Enders. They had thirteen children. The eleventh, Seth Damon Seiders, was the author's grandfather. Sarah died in 1914 and Joseph in 1918. Daniel Seal's mother died at age 81 in 1884. With the exception of Daniel and her daughter Ann Jane who died at age 7, all of Catharine Miller Seal's children lived long lives.

The cost of the war was enormous. In monetary terms, the price was approximately $7 billion dollars, over $75 billion in today's dollars. In human terms, the cost was staggering. In 1860, the U.S., population was just under 30 million. For many years, the war's official death toll has hovered around 620,000, though this number wouldn't have included soldiers who were mustered out, then died at home from wounds or illness. Sarah Enders' brother, Joseph, would have been one example. He died about a month after returning home from service with the 172nd Pennsylvania Drafted Militia, probably from a disease contracted during the war. More recently, historians have revised the death toll upward, closer to 750,000. Over 275,000 Union and over 194,000 Confederate soldiers were wounded and a large portion of these died within a few years of the war's end. Nearly every American alive in 1865 would have been touched by loss or wounding of loved ones.

Revisionist historians have tried to make the Civil War nothing more than a fight to end slavery, though the institution existed on both sides throughout the duration of the conflict. Because it remained in the Union, Daniel's home state of Missouri was exempt from the Emancipation Proclamation of 1863. Slavery continued there until a state convention approved an ordinance abolishing slavery on January 11, 1865. Kentucky and Delaware were two other slave states that remained loyal to the Union and were also exempt from the Emancipation Proclamation. The ratification of the 13th Amendment to the U.S. Constitution in December 1865 brought an end to slavery in those two states, eight months after the end of the war. Delaware ceremonially ratified the 13th Amendment in 1901, though Kentucky did not do so until 1976. The causes of the war have been debated for over 150 years and likely the debate will continue. Regardless of the opinions you might have, certainly we should be aware that the common foot soldier on both sides of the conflict suffered great hardships and witnessed horrible scenes too gruesome to contemplate for the majority of readers.

War has been a part of human history from Old Testament times through the present. The death and destruction of the Civil War certainly could have been avoided. In any case, we must realize that sin is the reason behind any war. Of course, it's very discouraging to see the horrible effects, but thankfully, God has provided a remedy for sin. We live in a fallen world, but though faith in Jesus Christ, we can have peace and joy, and the promise of an eternity where sin and suffering will be gone forever.

Appendix

MISSOURI SOLDIERS (1861-1865) WAR BETWEEN THE STATES

Lt
Pvt.

SEALS   DANIEL

SURNAME   GIVEN NAME   RANK

Co. "E"   1st Mo. Vol. Cav.   C.S.A.   Capt. Holland

SERVICE

April 15, 1862   Ark.

DATE ENLISTED   PLACE OF ENLISTMENT

DATE   PLACE   KILLED   PAROLED   DISCHARGED

CONFIRMATION OF RECORD:

Elected 2nd Lt. March 1, 1864. Battles:-Blue Mills,
Lexington, Bentonville, Elk Horn, Farmington, Iuka,
Corinth, Baker's Creek, Big Black, Vicksburg where
wounded, New Hope Church, Ga., Killed in battle of
Kenesaw Mt., Ga., June 20, 1864.

Muster Roll on file Adj. Gen. Office--Jefferson City, Mo.

Nat.   Pennsylvania
Res.   Buchanan Co., Mo.   MISSOURI STATE ARCHIVES
                        CERTIFICATE OF WAR SERVICE
                         Civil War - Confederate

137

Declaration for Pension.
Act of May 11, 1912
~~Act of February 6, 1907.~~

☞ *The Pension Certificate should not be forwarded with the Application.* ☜

☞ **INSTRUCTIONS.**—This form may be used for Original Pension or Increase of Pension. Declaration and testimony in support of same to be executed before some officer of a court of record having custody of its seal, a notary public, justice of the peace, or other officer authorized to administer oaths for general purposes. If such officer is not required by law to have and use a seal, his official character, signature and term of office must be certified by the proper State, county, or city officer under his official seal, unless such certificate has been filed in the Bureau of Pensions for general reference.

State of Dauphin , County of Dauphin , ss :

On this 18th day of May , A. D. one thousand nine hundred and twelve,

personally appeared before me, a Justice of the Peace within and for the County and

State aforesaid, Joseph Seiders, , who being duly sworn according to law,

declares that he is 71 years of age, and a resident of Lykens,

County of Dauphin , State of Penna. ; and that he is

the identical person who was **ENROLLED** at Harrisburg Pa. under the name of

Joseph Seiders, on the 22nd day of October , 1862,

as a Private , in Co, A, 172, Regt, Penna drafted Militia,
Here state rank and company and regiment in the Army, or vessel if in the Navy

in the service of the United States, in the civil War, and was **HONORABLY DISCHARGED** at
State name of War, Civil or Mexican

Harrisburg Pa., (July 31, 1863) on the 31st day of July , 1863,

That he also served as a Private in Co, H, 187th Regt Pa, Vol, from 29th
Here give a complete statement of all other service, if any

day of March 1864 to August 3rd 1865,

That he was not employed in the military or naval service of the United States otherwise than as stated above.

That his personal description at enlistment was as follows : Height, 5 feet 4 inches ; complexion, light ; color of eyes, light ; color of hair, light ; that his occupation was Farmer

that he was born March 12th , 18 41 at Dauphin County, Pa.

That his several places of residence since leaving the service have been as follows : always lived
State the date of each change

in Dauphin County,
as nearly as possible

That he is NOW a pensioner. That he has XXXX heretofore applied for pension

under ~~certificate No~~ 196,547,
If a pensioner, the certificate number only need be given. If not, give the number of the former application, if one was made

That he makes this Declaration for the purpose of being placed on the Pension-Roll of the United States, under the provisions of the ~~Act of February 6, 1907~~ Act of May 11, 1912

~~He also appoints, with full power of substitution and revocation,~~

~~DAVIS M. MELLON, POTTSVILLE, PENNA.~~

his true and lawful attorney , to prosecute his claim, and requests and directs that he be allowed and paid, upon the issuance of a Certificate, or thereafter, such fee as may be hereafter provided by law, NOT EXCEEDING TEN DOLLARS.

His post-office address is Lykens, County of Dauphin

State of Pennsylvania,

Claimant's signature *Joseph Seiders*

Attest 1. *Joseph Dunlap*
2. *Henry Weigelt*
Two witnesses who can write must sign here

Genealogical Information

Joseph S. Enders: 1841 -1863

Son of George Enders and Susannah Fetterhoff

Brother of Sarah Ellen Enders

(Died one month after returning home from the war)

Sarah Ellen Enders: 1847 – 1914

Daughter of George Enders and Susannah Fetterhoff

Wife of Joseph Seiders

Christina Jane Enders Miller: 1779 – 1851

Daughter of Philip Christian Enders and Anna Apolonia Degen (German immigrants)

Wife of John Miller (1778 – 1849)

Catharine Miller Seal: 1803 – 1884

Daughter of John Miller and Christina Jane Enders

Wife of Daniel Seal (1801 – 1852)

Mary Jane Miller Seiders: 1810 – 1872

Daughter of John Miller and Christina Jane Enders

Wife of Henry Seiders (1806 -1877)

Daniel Seal, Jr.: 1842 – 1864

Son of Daniel Seal and Catharine Miller

(Killed at Kennesaw Mountain, Georgia June 20, 1864)

Israel Seiders: 1838 - 1904

Son of Henry Seiders and Mary Jane Miller

Joseph Seiders: 1841 - 1918

Son of Henry Seiders and Mary Jane Miller

(Wounded at Petersburg, Virginia June 18, 1864)

William Henry Seiders: 1843 - 1889

Son of Henry Seiders and Mary Jane Miller

About the Author

Russell J. Ottens was born in 1954 on Long Island, NY, the son of Marguerite I. Seiders Ottens and Harry Ottens. He's retired from a long career with the Univ. of Georgia's Department of Entomology.

His wife is the former Mary Elizabeth Bagley. They have been blessed with three wonderful children and three lovely grandchildren.